BARBARIAN HERO

Michelle Janene

BARBARIAN HERO

Michelle Janene

STRONG TOWER
PRESS

Sacramento, CA

Strong Tower Press
Sacramento, CA
StrongTowerPress.com

Cover Art by: Whetstone Designs
Images: DespositPhotos.com
ISBN: 978-1-942320-19-7

For thus says the Lord GOD:
"Indeed I Myself will search for My sheep
and seek them out.

I will seek what was lost
and bring back what was driven away,
bind up the broken and
strengthen what was sick."
Ezekiel 34:11 and 16

CHAPTER

ONE

114 AD

Shrieks of terror echoed off the marble walls, tumbled around the columns, plummeted to the mosaic floor, then fell silent. Death had invaded the villa. As lives were cut down, Salomeh sat frozen on her knees in a seldom-used chamber.

Garbled barbaric speech assaulted her ears as much as the death cries of those within the house. Heavy boots pounded the tiles filling the villa with thunder. Cries for mercy were cut short. Challenges ended quickly. Soon they would come for her. Only a few more rooms and they would discover this hiding place.

Four other household slaves took shelter with Salomeh. Their muttered cries called out to Jupiter, their supreme god, and Vesta the goddess of the hearth. Their words, jumbled by their tears, went unanswered as death continued to advance. They pleaded to Jupiter to save them, but he did not.

Salomeh kept silent in prayer to the only God she knew could help, Yeshua, Christus. Head bowed and eyes closed to the horror around her, she sought His comfort. *My Savior, I come to You now. Forgive me for any uncleanness and take me into Your arms.* Even in the chaos, peace engulfed her.

The door to their chamber banged open.

She did not move.

Stomped steps were drown out by screams for mercy.

One by one the cries around her silenced.

She waited for the deathblow to come.

Unintelligible shouts erupted near the doorway. The footsteps retreated from her. Two voices vied with one another in an incomprehensible tirade of words. Something thudded into the wall. Metal rang against metal. The argument grew—the metal echoed more insistently.

A groan.

Then silence.

Heavy footsteps crossed the room toward her.

Salomeh, eyes still clamped closed, waited. Her heart pounded in her ears, but she remained still. *I am ready, Lord.*

A hand crushed hers still grasped in prayer. Her eyes shot open. A bare-chested man tightened a bloody sash around her wrists and yanked her to her feet. The blond warrior towered above her. He did not pause. His hand on the other end of the tether jerked her forward.

She stumbled at the sudden movement. Trying to gain her footing, she slid on the slick floor. Frantically, she looked about the room. Blood stained the mortar between the mosaic tiles. It ran down the marble walls. She stepped over the body of a fallen barbarian. His eyes open staring at nothing and his innards spilling from a gut wound.

Salomeh turned away as bile burned the back of her throat. Stomach sour, she gazed on her master, split from throat to navel and laid across the low dining table like some gruesome main course. Salomeh's captor jerked her forward. She fell to the cool titles and wretched. She prayed the purging of her stomach would empty her mind of all she saw.

It didn't.

He waited as her stomach emptied of its content and yet continued to heave. Guttural shouts filled the house now adding to the clank and jingle of all Master's possessions being stripped from within.

She fought for breath. *Yeshua, help me.* Tears poured from her eyes as she looked at all those dead in the villa. *Christus, they did not know You. Have mercy.* Her deep sobs stuttered her breaths. *I have failed to share You, my God. They are lost because of me.*

The man yanked her to her feet and raked the hide of a dead creature across her mouth. He stood over a head taller than her, and his blue eyes pierced her until she quaked under his gaze. His thick beard was darker than his hair. The fair skin of his bare chest lay covered in streaks and droplets of blood. His great heaving breaths warmed her clammy skin. Every muscle lay carved as though he were a sculpture of a Roman hero.

But this man was no champion. He broke into Master's home, helped kill everyone within, and now held her tied with a bloody sash from a fallen slave. Not a hero but a nightmare. Salomeh shuddered at what he planned for her.

A bellow from the atrium caused him to turn, and his mane of hair brushed her cheek. He shouted a reply and pulled her toward the center of the villa.

They met a dozen fair-skinned warriors of equal size near the pool where rainwater collected through the opening in the ceiling. It rippled but gave no reflection from its red depths. Once, it had been a source of fresh water from the heavens; now it mirrored the rest of the house—dead and of no value to anyone.

Again, her stomach heaved. Tears streaked her cheeks. A strangled cry at seeing the body of her mistress escaped from her throat.

Another attacker rose his sword above her. Sunlight through the shattered door glinted off the metal where it could be seen through the blood.

Yes, Christus. Take me. Do not let me see more of this horror—or a worse fate befall me.

The man who held her fetter used his fearsome blade to smash against the falling sword. Metal rang against the blood-splattered wall. Her abductor blocked the strike that would have released her from this life. He stood between her and a quick death. Words were exchanged. Her captor pushed the other man away and stomped to the door. Salomeh staggered after him. Laughter followed—sneering, mocking, scornful.

Salomeh stumbled behind her captor. Logic fled. She should run—try to escape. All she could manage was to put one foot in front of the other. Hope could not be found, and freedom lay beyond her reach. Her head dropped and touched her collar. Red spatter stained her tunic. Why spare her? What did he want?

He turned, causing her to stumble into him. His already guttural words muttered over his tight lips and through his clenched jaw. His eyes narrowed, watching the men exit the house behind her, then his gaze shifted to her. His features softened. He shook his head, tossing his golden locks about his shoulder. More of the pink of his lips could be seen between his beard and moustache. He appeared alien to her, so unlike the clean-shaven men of Rome who kept their hair short. He continued to stare as though trying to decide what to do with her. His brow arched and a few words came her way.

She did not know what he wanted, but he turned back and pulled her along as the others stomped past them laden down with their spoils.

The beast at the end of her tether didn't carry a thing—other than her lead.

Dragged away from the home she had lived in since Master was ordered here by Rome, Salomeh looked around. She alone survived. She saw a glow on her abductor's back. The air filled with ash. She turned her head. The villa burned.

CHAPTER

TWO

Salomeh staggered to keep up with her long-legged captor as he dragged her through the brush. Her short slave's tunic and sandals offered little protection from the rough branches and thorns that slapped against her and tore at her flesh. Her captor could only be one of the feared Germani soldiers who constantly threatened the Roman boarder. Heedless of her plight, he strolled, in his fur-topped boots and coarse braccae covering his legs, as though in a marbled hall.

She stumbled, jerking him to a halt as she fell. Her legs were caked with blood, and dirt clung to her sandals and legs. She didn't rise so he stomped back to her. *Yeshua, let him kill me now. I can't go on.*

He hovered over her.

She shook her head and pointed her thumb at her throat—the sign given by the public to end a gladiator's life. *Understand. Please, end this.*

He shook his head, barked an order, and jerked her to her feet.

She waivered, unable to move forward.

He stepped to her, and suddenly she hung over his shoulder like a sack of vegetables. She bounced against him—her stomach taking the brunt of it—as he raced to take up the last position in the line of retreating attackers.

As Salomeh dangled, she glanced past her capture's hip and saw several of his people turn at his approach. They sneered, and said something that caused him to tighten his grip across her legs until her toes tingled.

Too tired and weak to get free, Salomeh gave up and let thoughts of Master fill her. The once powerful Servius Roscius Curio had fallen from the Roman Senate's favor. He took a post on the Limes in hopes of rebuilding his name and reputation.

The memory of Mistress Decima's tears again filled Salomeh's thoughts bring to mind her sobbed words. "You cannot take us to live so near those Germanic barbarians. We will be killed, or worse."

At the time, Salomeh couldn't think of what would be worse than death by a savage's hand, but now she feared she would soon find out.

Before they even left Rome, whispers of raids by the Germanic tribes circulated among the household slaves. But Master Curio promised, "The Limes have been built to protect Roman citizens from any trouble. The forts stand everywhere. Trouble could not come without a legion being immediately at hand to run the vermin back to their holes."

Trouble had come. But not one Roman soldier had arrived to aid them.

The blond captor stopped and released her. She fell to her backside unable to find her footing fast enough. A river lay before them. Most of the men were undressed and entering the water to scrub themselves free of Roman blood.

Heat flooded her face and Salomeh turned her back to them. Even in the public baths of Rome, men and women did not bathe together. Each was assigned a time to come—citizens in the morning, slaves in the middle of the day and then citizens could return in the evening. She hid herself from viewing these barbarians, but the blond at the end of her tether jerked her to her feet and led her toward the water. She fought him, pulled against her bindings, and tried again to sit. He picked her up and threw her into the water.

She came up sputtering to the laughter of the others. Salomeh did her best to swim a couple of awkward strokes with her bound hands. The current tugged at her swirling around her legs in stinging waves. Sand brushed against her toes as solid bottom scraped under her hard leather soles. Almost in the middle of the river, the water to her chin, she found a wide enough place to stand and again turned her back on the naked men.

Shouts arose behind her. Salomeh spun to see three warriors swimming toward her. She struggled to remain on her perch on the rock but fell back into the current at their advance. She flipped over and pulled herself through the water kicking out behind her. At her second kick, a hand seized her ankle and pulled her under the surface. She came up coughing to more laughter.

The man who grabbed her pressing himself against her his hand tracing up her leg.

She screamed and tried to pry herself free, but his arm encircled her pinning her bound hands between them.

A roar burst from the shore, and her blond kidnapper hurled

himself into the water at the man holding her. Dunked again, Salomeh fought to free herself and surface.

The splashing and yelling of the grappling men nearby drowned out her coughing.

Her attacker vanished under the waves. The three others turned their attention back on Salomeh calling out messages she didn't want to understand.

Sink. Drown. Go to the Savior and be free. She kicked away into the strongest part of the current and stopped fighting.

Her new master burst to the surface behind the one who had grabbed her and struck him in the head with a rock. The man slumped and fell to his back. The others rushed to tend him, and the victor swam straight for her.

His eyes searched Salomeh. He raised his hands above the water mimicking her bound wrists by pressing his together. She mirrored his action. He collected the tether in his firm grasp and swam closer motioning for her to come near.

She shook her head. Salomeh wanted no part of whatever he wanted to do.

He looked to those watching them and seized her about the waist—though not as tight as the other man. He pressed her back to his chest. Turning his back to the opposite shore he swam until his feet found solid ground. Standing with rivulets of water streaming off them, he set her on the rocky shore—unfortunately missing several softer clumps of grass. Face buried in her hands, she let the tears come. *Yeshua, my God, save me.*

Salomeh did not have long to wallow. While the saturated tunic still clung to her, the Germani pulled her up, and they walked again. The man he struck with the rock leaned on one of his companions. Her captor watched, maintaining a distance from them.

They must have covered over three-dozen milias. Her feet scraped along the ground. She panted for breath. Her parched lips clung to her teeth. They crested a ridge and, through the trees, she caught glimpses of rustic huts.

Close to forty of them spread out in a small clearing nestled in a long, narrow hollow. The blond walked through the middle of the settlement. Women turned and sneered—calling out words Salomeh praised God she could not comprehend. She sidestepped where one spit on the ground and ducked under the thrown remains of a dinner. The man at the end of her lead shouted at them, yanked her closer, and continued to the last hut on the edge of the others. It was half the size of every other dwelling, though not particularly small, and sat off on its own. It was just large enough for him and his animals.

Her captor jerked up on the latch and threw open the rough wood door. He shoved her inside. She fell, landing on her hands and knees on the dirt floor. The stench of animal waste overwhelmed. Bile washed her tongue. The musty smell of thatch overhead and the mud walls made the stench worse. Could she find the river again?

There was a sleeping area with a mat on the floor covered in a fur. A few chests sat against the back and right walls. She now sat in an open space about the size of the sleeping area on her right that contained the only piece of furniture—a table against the front wall. To her left, she saw a roped off space equal to the rest of his home littered with animal droppings. A larger door led out the back of the house.

The wood door clattered closed. He secured the latch and stalked toward her.

She tried to crawl away but, with her hands tied and every muscle in revolt, she didn't manage to move far.

He scooped Salomeh in his arms and carried her to a low mat filled with straw. Plopping her down on his bedroll, he rent a small tear in her tunic up from the hem.

She screamed.

He nodded, waving his hands to encourage her.

Planting bound hands against his hard bare chest, she pushed him away.

He raised his hand, palm open, to strike.

Salomeh cringed, eyes closed.

The slap of skin against skin rang in her ears, but no sting came with it. Salomeh dared open her eyes and realized he had slapped his own flesh. What was he doing? Did he mean to inflict pain, but missed? Scattered thoughts flopped around like a dying fish on the shore.

He frowned, his thick blond brows drew together. He lunged. She shrieked, tears cascading over her cheeks. A stuttered breath tumbled out as she bit her knuckles to stifle the panic.

He shook his head, removed her hand, touched a tear as it escaped, and traced it down her cheek. He drew another and another nodding at her. He wanted her to cry. She fought bending to his wishes, so he rent another tear up the side of her tunic.

Sobs came against her will.

Another slap of his own flesh. Another lunge.

More screams escaped against her will accompanied by more cries.

He sat back on his heels and smiled. He drew more tears down her cheeks encouraging her to keep crying.

He moved to the other side of the hut as she curled on her side and cried until sleep claimed her.

CHAPTER

THREE

Cold. Stinging. A rough hand clamped around her foot. Salomeh jerked and tried to sit up. Water caressed her foot. Her abductor put his hand on her shoulder pushing her down. His touch was gentle as he scrubbed her feet until they were clean. He rubbed an ointment over them and into the deep cuts and scratches in her legs. He brushed away some hair, which had fallen from her braid, and rubbed more salve into a cut on the side of her neck using his thumb.

He cleaned his hands on the filthy animal skin he had worn over his shoulder during the attack. Putting one hand under her head, he placed a cup to her lips. The sour beer bit at her dry tongue, and she coughed against it.

She tried to push it away.

He refused, shaking his head, and again placed the cup to her lips pouring more slowly. Salomeh's head spun, and her vision blurred. He laid her back down, letting his fingers trail over her face.

She coughed, choking on the smoke. Salomeh's hands clamped over her ears, teeth grinding against the screams. She looked down.

She stood in a pool of blood rising up to her waist. Her hands dripped with the gooey red liquid.

She screamed.

Crying, Salomeh sat up rubbing away the sleep. Where was she? A sheep bleated. Her hand brushed over a dirt floor. A blond man, bare to the waist came toward her. She blinked. A scream burst from her throat as his hand fastened over her ankle, stopping her from crawling away. This nightmare did not end like the last. The man still held her. This wasn't a dream. She was still a captive in a disgusting hut that also housed animals.

His hands rose with slow purpose, and he ripped another gash in her tunic, this time down the neck a few inches.

She screamed and hit his hands away.

He smiled, tracing his finger down her cheeks.

Salomeh shook and pushed at him again. "I will not cry on demand for you."

He gripped Salomeh's wrists, bolts of pain shot up her shoulders. She cried out. He jerked her close, and released her. Again fabric tore.

Tears turned to frantic sobs. They boiled up like a dreadful brew. Bile washed over her tongue.

As before, he sat back and smiled.

Her face felt as though it were ablaze. She pulled her legs to her chest, wrapped her arms around them, pressed her cheeks to her knees, and wept. Lungs burned. Sides ached. Still the tears came—as much from her captive status as from the kindness her captor showed her.

As she quieted, Salomeh again felt his tender touch on her feet.

He applied more ointment. The thick cream from the night before left behind healing scabs. He reapplied it to the cuts on her legs, neck, and the welts on her wrists left by the sash. Until he held her hands, she hadn't realized she was no longer bound. Next, he lifted the cup again, but she pulled away, sticking her tongue out.

A low rumble of laughter tumbled out of him. He pointed to her treated wounds and then to the cup. He did it twice before she understood, like the ointment, the drink was medicinal.

Salomeh took it and sipped.

He sat back staring at her. His hand reached out, and he pushed the cup up again.

She drank a little more. His image danced, blurring and solidifying in waves.

Placing his hand flat against his chest, he spoke a single word. "Volkard." He patted his chest. "Vol-kard," he said more slowly and put his hand, palm out, facing her. He tapped his chest, "Volkard," and moved his hand to her.

"Salomeh," she whispered.

His hand dropped to his lap. "Salomeh." He rolled her name around on his tongue a few times until he said it correctly. His features shifted, and the stern warrior surfaced again. He pointed to the space around them and the dirt below them. "Volkard, Salomeh." Next he pointed toward the door and beyond and shook his head. He repeated it, pointing inside, "Volkard, Salomeh," and outside, "Nien."

She struggled to keep her eyes open as the drink took hold.

He grabbed her by the chin, startling her to alertness for a moment longer. He again pointed outside and put his hand over her mouth.

She pulled from him, the medicine making her sway with the effort. She pointed around them, and repeated, "Volkard, Salomeh." Then she pointed to the door and covered her mouth with both hands and lowered her head.

Her hands dropped to her lap. Her eyes would not open. She felt Volkard's hands guide her back to lay on his mat.

When next she woke, the animals were gone and so was Volkard. She stared up at the thatch and tree beams holding it aloft as she considered the unusual man. He'd saved her. But why? Volkard killed one of his own rather than allow her to die. He wounded another to stop her assault. Yet he wanted everyone to believe he had hurt her in the same manner.

None of it made any sense. Salomeh's head rumbled with a dull ache. *What would You have me do, Lord?*

The first thing to come to mind was a passage from the sacred Jewish Torah, which gave provision for a man taking a wife from among his captives. He could bring her home, shave her head, and after he kept her for a month, she was his wife. She greatly doubted that Volkard knew of the holy writings, but was that what this was somehow? Did Volkard intend to take her as his wife? If so, why make everyone believe he had assaulted her against her will? She shuddered at the idea.

Again, she asked the Lord what He wished of her. Her prayer brought to mind a conversation she had in the market with another believer years ago. Maritsa had come from Armenia at the same time as Salomeh. They had both been sold in Rome to different families, but they looked for each other anytime their chores took them to the common areas.

"Salomeh, you must pray for your master and be the most honorable and upright slave. It brings honor to God and blessings to you and your master," Maritsa had said.

"Why would I pray for them?"

"Do you not remember the lessons taught to us when we were children? 'Submit yourselves for the Lord's sake to every human authority.' And in Paul's blessed letters he told us, 'Slaves, obey your earthly masters with respect and fear, with your whole heart, as you obey Christus. Obey not only to win favor but to do the will of God from your heart.' The Lord will reward each one for whatever good they do, no matter if we are slave or free. This comes from God, Salomeh. And remember Joseph? While he served as a slave in Potiphar's home, Potiphar grew wealthy and all his businesses did well, all because of Joseph."

Salomeh had tried to pray for Master, but all she saw in him was another Roman like the ones who laid siege to her homeland under Emperor Trajan. Starvation claimed both Mother and her sister; and finally, Father died protecting her. She would have died then too, if the Romans had not declared victory and added Armenia into the Roman Empire. But they had taken her back to Rome as a slave.

I can't pray for Master. I won't pray for him or any Roman.

That had been her vow. If she couldn't pray for a Roman, could she find it in her heart to pray for a Germani barbarian? The crisscrossed thatch stared back at her with no answers.

CHAPTER

FOUR

The rough dirt floor cut into Salomeh's skin as she knelt. Guilt drove her to her knees after staring at the ceiling. But prayer wouldn't come right away. The stench of manure drew her thoughts to the filth of her surroundings. How could she now view Rome as heaven when compared to this place. Hate festered, twisting her heart and her thoughts. Peace fled. Carried off from one imprisonment to another—forever someone's captive. Only one thing would change everything.

"Christus, I would not pray for Master Curio. I harbored a hatred of all Romans deep in my heart. Forgive me." Tears slid down her cheeks, hot against cold skin. "Master treated me fairly." The thought of her time in Curio's household overwhelmed her and she dropped down to sit on her heels. "Curio was never cruel. He never forced me to his bed—a fate so many women have suffered in Roman hands. But I would never pray for him as Maritsa told me," the words choked on her tears.

The guilt pressed on Salomeh's shoulders and threatened to flatten her into the floor. Lungs struggled for air; eyes flew open as she panted for breath.

Volkard squatted inside the door staring. His head tipped, and blond hair with a slight wave through its lengths brushed past his shoulders. Bushy brows pulled together over faint blue eyes. The short tunic now covering his broad chest strained against his bulging muscles.

Her hands dropped to her lap.

Still he stared—his gaze running over her like a gentle caress.

She pointed to the heavens, "Christus."

He nodded, stood, and walked around the hut pointing at the hammers carved into many of the posts holding up the structure sheltering them. "Thor."

Hands lying still, Salomeh's head bowed, as her heart cried out. *I will not worship his pagan god.*

Volkard knelt beside her, taking both her hands, he clasped them together as she had done as she prayed. "Christus," he said letting go.

She let them drop.

He placed them again in the mode of prayer, saying more insistently, "Christus."

He wanted Salomeh to pray? To her God?

"Christus," he said again nodding.

She inclined her head, eyes closed. "Christus, I have been brought here by this man, Volkard. He wishes I pray to You. I do not know his need, but You know, my God. I ask for Your blessings to be upon him." The words came in a fluid stream and not strangled, as she feared they would. The pleasure of her God filled her, loosening her tongue to pray with genuine concern for this brute of a man. "Watch over all he has and all he does. May there be a way for him to learn about You in his own tongue. May there come a day when Volkard calls upon the name of Christus as his God. In Your most holy name, amen."

When Salomeh looked once more, Volkard again squatted near the door staring at her. His lips could not be seen amongst the thick hair on his face. His eyes were narrowed, but he did not glare at her. His gaze continued to search hers.

Salomeh struggled to stand. Her legs stiff and feet sore, she quavered. How did she make him understand she prayed only for his good? She swayed and wobbled forward.

The dark-blond hair around his mouth pulled down. He stood and watched her every move.

She crept toward him, feet dragging, breaths skipping. Her hand trembled as she laid it over his heart. "Christus," she whispered, trying to smile.

His heart pounded under her fingertips. Volkard's gaze rested on her hand for a long moment. He stepped back leaving air between them. His gaze became hard.

Salomeh's breath caught, and her stomach grumbled.

He turned on his heel, smacked at a hammer carving, "Thor," he grunted and disappeared out the door. It slammed closed.

Salomeh sighed, staggered back toward his bedroll, and knelt again in prayer.

He returned, dropped a round loaf of dark bread on Salomeh's lap, and placed a cup next to her. He walked back to the door but stopped before opening it, pointed at her and then the floor. She was to stay inside. That much was clear. She nodded and he disappeared. The sheer terror of venturing out among his people would not have allowed her to leave.

Salomeh ate the bread and drank the beer. Her stomach quieted, but how her mouth watered for fruits and wine. "Lord, I viewed my days in the Roman villa as a prison. I did not know the luxuries I indulged in every day. The privileges and ease of my life with the Romans I scorned, because of the lack of my freedom. Christus, I ask You to create in me a grateful heart. Even here in this dirt hut shared with the animals." She wrinkled her nose at the pervasive smell. "May I find something everyday to be thankful for, my Lord."

Looking around the waddle and daub structure with its dirt floor, Salomeh prayed for something—anything—to praise God for. She scratched at her leg, scraping some of the dried ointment from a healing wound. As her hand dropped away, she tipped over the empty cup.

Salomeh's head rose to the heavens she could not see through the thick thatch, "Christus, I thank You for Volkard. He has protected, cared, and provided for me. Thank You."

Focusing on something besides what she had lost—family in Armenia, her comfortable life in Rome—helped peace return to her spirit. Salomeh moved to the straw bed, curled up, and fell asleep.

She dreamed of a simple structure with a wood floor, plaster walls, and vellum windows. A figure filled the doorway, but the bright sun behind held the face in shadows.

CHAPTER

FIVE

"Salomeh?"

She stirred at her name on the Germani's tongue.

"Salomeh?"

She opened her eyes to see Volkard squatting beside her. In his hands he held two items. He pushed one toward her. It was a pair of course braccae.

He waved at her to put them on.

She held the men's leg coverings in her hands looking at them. Salomeh—no matter the dire state of things—had never dressed in trousers.

"Salomeh," Volkard pulled the blanket from her lap. He pulled the braccae from her hands and moved to her feet as though he intended to dress her.

She snatched the men's garment back and waved him away. He didn't move, and she pointed out the door with the braccae clutched to her chest. It was like trying to pick up and move a villa. Salomeh took his hands and put them over his eyes.

A low chuckle rumbled through his chest as he stood and turned toward the animal pen.

The rough fabric scraped up her legs. She drew the waist tight tying the braided cord as he turned around.

He twisted them around her waist, straightened them, and knelt at her feet. Taking a knife from his belt he cut off the excess. Even the Germani women were tall. Next, he held out the other item he'd brought. A pair of fur topped boots. He held the first one out, and she slipped her foot inside. Warm, soft, fuzziness caressed her foot, but the boot was big. Her foot slipped around inside.

Volkard jostled the ill-fitting footwear. He stood and rubbed his hand over his chin. He turned, muttering as he walked around looking at his few belongs. Snatching up the skin he had draped over his shoulder when he came to the villa, he cut off a piece. Removing the boot, Volkard stuffed the fur inside the bottom of the boot, removed it, trimming the hide's shape, and replaced it. After doing this several times for each boot, he held them out for her to try again.

They fit much better, and Salomeh trusted they would not slip off every time she took a step.

He knelt and tucked the legs of the braccae, in the top of the boots. He stood and walked around her with an appraising stare. After a few circuits, he pulled out the thong that had held her hair up and neat. He ran his fingers in her hair and mussed it more. He loosened the sash at her waist and tugged up her tunic so it spilled over continuing to dishevel her appearance.

Salomeh's breath caught in her throat as he increased the rips in what was left of her tunic—several up from the hem, and the one more down at the neck. Air wafted over her exposed collarbone and shoulder raising the gooseflesh on her arms.

Volkard circled her again and nodded. He stopped directly before her and huffed. He clasped her by both shoulders and gave her a light shake. Volkard's gaze bore into her soul. He pointed to her, to himself, and the door.

He meant to take her outside—among his tribe again.

His hand waved across the expanse around them, and then he touched his eyes. They grew wide as he stared at her and circled.

The tribe would be watching what he did and how she behaved.

She lowered her head and cowered, flinching at his every move. She even dropping at his feet. When Salomeh raised her head to look at him again and found him nodding—a small smile crinkled the hair at the corner of his lips.

Volkard brought her back up to her feet and gripped her shoulders again. He paused to stare at her for a moment. He raised his right hand as though to strike her right cheek with the back of his hand.

She gulped air and stiffened prepared for the blow.

He shook his head and brought the hand down toward her face with slow deliberate purpose. As it touched her skin, he pushed her face aside. Grabbing her chin, he turned her back to look at him, a brow arched high.

She nodded.

He raised his hand and repeated the motion. This time Salomeh moved with him without any prodding. He nodded once more, and released her other shoulder. With hand raised yet again, they went through the motions of his attack several more times each time increasing the speed. At last satisfied the strike would look good without actually hurting her, he straightened his shirt, gave her a curt nod, and moved to the door.

"Volkard," she whispered before he led them outside.

He whirled, concern pinching his features.

Summoning her courage, Salomeh reached for his hand and brought it to the back of her head closing his fingers around her hair.

He pulled his hand away and shook his head.

Salomeh tried again. Using her own hand, she took a clump of hair and pulled it away from her scalp and shook her head showing him she was not hurt. Making at fist around the hair, she put it against her head and pushed taking a staggering step toward him.

He frowned, turned to look at the closed door, and at last grunted. He reached for the ends of her hair, grabbed up a small handful, and pressed his fist against the back of her head near the crown. He looked at her, his gaze searching her face.

She nodded and took a step closer.

He placed his other hand on the door and pushed it open.

CHAPTER

SIX

The sun hung low and only broke through the thick trees in a few locations as Volkard stomped into the open, giving all appearances of pulling Salomeh by the hair with him. They moved away from his hut. He pushed her toward the smoldering fire pit.

Under hooded eyes, Salomeh glimpsed those gathered about. Heads turned and every eye stared to see what he would do to her. Some spit on the ground. Others curled their lips in disgust. Many of the men smiled and tipped their chins to encourage Volkard's abusive actions.

Salomeh dropped to her knees as though shoved to the ground. She cowered there and flinched at his every movement.

Volkard moved so she sat between him and the villagers. He kicked at her and barked an order.

She fell away from him and cried out.

Laughter danced on the breeze at the cruelty they believed he dealt her.

He shouted at her again, and she raised her face to him. His hand rose. He paused for less than a heartbeat—his eyes locked with hers.

She gave him the slimmest of nods.

His hand flew.

Salomeh moved slower than they had practiced and a crack of skin against skin filled the silence. She moved quick enough to save herself the worst of the pain, but she knew the contact had to be heard.

Volkard stifled a gulp of air.

Covering her face with her hand, she crumpled to the ground. Salomeh pinched her cheek where he'd struck her to make it redden even more. She crawled to his feet and made to be kissing his boots as she cried.

Cheers and laughter rewarded Volkard's abuse.

Volkard filled his hand with her hair again, and he hesitated for that imperceptible instant once more.

She rose under his hold until she sat tall on her knees.

He crouched before her, scowl deep on his face, but his eyes were filled with worry as they searched hers.

She blinked slowly and nodded by the tiniest degree.

He pointed to the metal pot hanging over the coals and growled out orders she could only assume meant he wanted her to cook his meal.

Fear raced through her like a runaway horse. Staring at the foreign implement, she shuddered. How did she tell him she had never cooked a meal?

Free of his grasp, she picked up small logs and laid them on the fire. Her heart thundered in her ears. She was too young to help Mother before the Romans attacked, and other servants saw to the meal preparation in the villa. Salomeh cleaned. She could scour the pot, strip, and dress a bed, polish tile and metal pieces alike, but cook—she didn't even know where to begin.

Volkard dropped a hunk of meat in the pot.

She looked up to the first stars of the evening. *Thank You, Christus.*

He added more and dropped cut vegetables in with it. Next, he shoved a wooden spoon into her hand. He jerked away, gave a shout, held his knife high out of her reach and kicked at her again.

She crumpled with a whimper before rising to stir the stew. Volkard plopped down on a log grumbling and watched her as she tended the mixture over the hot flames.

As she worked, she stole glances at the others in the village. There were young and old, men and women, but none of them looked like Volkard. None were as fair as him, though they were all lighter skinned than the Romans or herself. They were tall as all the Germani were compared to the Romans, but Volkard still outreached even the tallest of them.

She wiped sweat from her brow on the back of her arm and continued to stir making sure to keep her head down.

Several gawked openly at her, and she noted their hair contained more brown than Volkard's which was almost white. His face was longer and thinner than theirs, as was his nose. *This is not his tribe,* she concluded.

He shoved a bowl into her hand drawing her from her musings. She filled it and passed it back to him with care. He ate his fill as she sat at his feet.

He made a big show of throwing out what remained in the pot before thrusting it into her hands and leading her, by the hair, to the stream where she washed it.

Hidden among the trees and away from most of the prying eyes, Salomeh relaxed. Cleaning a pot, she could do.

Volkard stood over her, his arms crossed, watching everything but her. Soon he had his hand in her hair, and they returned to his hut. Inside she saw his bowl—full of stew. How had he gotten it in here? He'd never come near the hut—had he?

Volkard tipped his head toward it, but still his arms remained firmly across his board chest.

She searched his face. Something was wrong. Her stomach fluttered.

He stomped toward her and raised his hand to backhand her again. He started to bring it down, raised it and repeated the motion several times before throwing up his hands and turning his back on her.

She clapped her hands together making him snap back around. She pointed to her ear and clapped again. Her ear and another clap. She pinched her cheek showing it to him. He snatched her chin and turned her face. Still holding her firmly in his hand his gaze searched her.

She laid her hand over his chest and whispered, "Volkard good."

His heart thundered under her fingers, his breaths became shallow, the dark centers of his eyes grew, consuming the blue. Volkard didn't move. His grip on her chin tightened until she couldn't move either. Sweat beaded on her skin.

CHAPTER

SEVEN

Volkard had jerked away, released her, pointed to the bowl with a grunted order, and left the hut.

As the days proceeded Salomeh saw less and less of him.

In a matter of only a couple of days, Salomeh grew restless. She needed something to occupy her. One would think that after suffering as a slave—working hard from sun up to sunset each day —she would relish doing nothing. "Christus, I know I begged for years on end to be freed of my slave bonds, but this is not what I had in mind. What am I doing here?"

With the items he had laying about the hut, she fashioned a rough broom—not a good one, but one that served her purpose. She mended one of his shirts and scooped all the foul straw in the animal pen toward the side door.

Volkard noted it as he returned with the beasts in the evening. He disposed of the soiled stubble outside and laid new straw.

The next morning, Volkard's cow created a ruckus pulling Salomeh from restless sleep well before the sun. The cow lowed insistently until Volkard rose to milk her.

Salomeh listened to him grumble sharp words she knew were curses as he moved a fat, rough-hewn three-legged seat and started to relieve the creature of her discomfort. Salomeh watched the muscles in his bare back work in the rhythmic motion, before she rose and drew near.

He startled when she plopped to her knees beside him. His rhythm stuttered for a moment.

She watched for several minutes before pointing to his hands and mimicked his actions.

His brows pulled together, but he released the cow and waved her to continue.

With one of her hands, she gripping the udder squeezed, and pulled down as he had.

The cow mooed and stomped her back hoof.

Salomeh tried again and the milk shot out hitting Volkard in the knee. She released the animal, and covering her mouth with her hands. Her gaze darted to him trying to read his face. What would he do?

He didn't yell or slap her. Instead he waved her to join him on the seat. She stood and his hands rested on her hips, and he pulled her down onto the rough wood. He pressed his chest against her back as his hands slid down her arms until his fingers covered hers. Covering her hands with his, he closed them gently on the udder once more. A zing of milk squirted into the bucket while he squeezed her hand and drew down.

Salomeh giggled at the success.

Volkard worked her other hand to the same result. As the motion went back and forth between her hands, she continued, but he reached up and brushed her hair aside.

His whiskers tickled the nape of her neck and the scoop below her ear. His breath warmed her skin and gooseflesh rose on her arms. His other hand slipped around her waist just below her bosom.

She could not tell if the heart pounding was in her chest or against her back. A fiery warmth melted her at his touch.

A low rumble vibrated through him like a growl. His hold tightened on her.

She placed her hand on his knee, and struggled to release a word. "Volkard?"

He jerked, and as though turned to stone, he didn't move. Without warning, he leapt from the seat. Perched only on the front edge of the stool, she toppled forward and landed under the cow. He muttered, what she again assumed were curses, and stomped toward the door. He hit a carved hammer on the post on his way. The name Thor was distinguishable in his jumbled words, and he threw his hands up to the heavens. The door banged behind him.

Salomeh righted the seat and took her place again. She managed to fill the bucket with the warm white liquid, but she could not shake the sensations Volkard had aroused in her. He awakened feelings within her that sent her to her knees in prayer. "Christus, I need Your guidance. Volkard stirs things within that frighten me. I do not know why he keeps me here or what will become of me in this village. Please, Christus, quiet the longing in my lonely heart."

Milking the cow became her new chore as she saw even less of Volkard. It became one of many she assigned herself to keep from falling into a stupor. The next couple of days, he didn't come anywhere near her. Whenever he returned at night, he would throw open the door and shout. Whether the word he bellowed was a simple 'come' or some vile name, she didn't know, but she would always hurry to the nightly meal preparations.

Salomeh couldn't tell if her efforts pleased or angered him because he spent so little time with her.

One night as he returned. she was using a smooth stick to scrape the filth from her arms and legs. It wasn't a proper strigl and she had no water, steam, or oil to aid in the process, but she could not stand how dirty she'd become. Since going to Rome she had never gone more than a day without a bath. Now here in this hut there wasn't even water, and Salomeh couldn't stand her own stench. Again, she shook her head at her longing for her former slave life.

He stared at her as she scraped the dirt away before they made their appearance at his fire pit, but this time as they returned from the river, he carried the pot full of water. They went inside, and he placed the pot on the floor, then threw a piece of cloth into it. When Salomeh didn't do anything with it, so he took out the damp cloth and ran it down her arm.

The cool water on her skin and his gentle touch set her insides fluttering and her skin to humming.

He drew nearer, and stood directly in front of her. With his gaze locked on her, he drew the cloth from her ear, down her neck, and across the torn collar of her tunic.

Her breath caught in her throat, and her mouth went dry. The center of his eyes grew larger until she could only see the black part, and she thought he might devour her. Salomeh tried to swallow, breathe, think. Her heart roared until she feared it would burst from her chest.

With a slow motion as though he was sap in winter, he raised the cloth again, this time brushing it across her cheek, along her quaking jaw, and over her parched lips. He caressed her lips again and leaned into her.

At once her breaths turned to shallow gasps.

He stared at her, his face only a breath from her own. Volkard hovered there his tongue wetting his own lips.

As her frantic gasps turned to panting, he blinked. Once, then again, and yet again. He looked at her as though he didn't know who she was. A slow sigh that almost hinted at a groan slipped from his lips. The cloth dropped from his hand on the rim of the pot, and she bent to retrieve it. The thought of the dirty fabric in the same pot as they prepared their meals, turned her stomach.

By the time she straightened, Volkard had disappeared out the door. He had not returned by the time sleep claimed her.

CHAPTER

EIGHT

How long had she been in Volkard's hut? Two weeks? Maybe.
There were no specific days set aside for going to the market,
annual festivals, or monthly events at the stadium. All she did was
sit in his hut for hours on end staring at a thatched roof and the
waddle and daub walls. She paced around her sleeping mat, and
threw her hands up in the air. She tried to think on something else.
It still amazed her that she found she truly missed being a Roman
slave.

She stomped to the door. Enough was enough. Time to get
out of here and back to some life somewhere. The door was not
bound shut. She could simply walk out.

Snickers danced in the silence as her hand touched the door.
She froze at the sounds. Being as still as possible she tried to look
around. Beams of light appeared and disappeared on the dirt floor.
They came through holes in the wall on her left. Eyes peeked
through the holes. How long had they been watching her? Could
she make it to the river? Her hand trembled on the door. Her eyes
clenched closed. Would not seeing help her decide? The brush of
the violating hand of the man in the river rushed over her skin.
Her eyes flew open. Salomeh shuddered, brushing her hands over

her to be rid of the memory.

She stared at the door as her breathing calmed. Volkard told her to stay inside and so far, everything he had done kept her safe. Giggles and soft cackles came from the holes again. She placed her hand on the door once more. Her heart nearly pounded out of her chest. Air refused to fill her lungs. Her eyes caught on the hammers carved on either side of the door. But Thor did not prevent her from leaving. Christus did. She dropped to her knees. *Lord, I do not know why, but I believe You want me to stay. Help me.*

Though no answers came to her pleas, she had a sense in her innermost being—she was here for Volkard as much as he was here for her. She hungered for so much more. Purpose, friendship, even a conversation with anyone would help.

That night, Salomeh worked a piece of leather she had noticed earlier in the day. Suddenly, the door banged open and Volkard charged at her, hand raised in a fist. She scrambled back from him. Air hissed through his locked jaws, and his chest heaved visibly under his shirt. His hand hovered in the air waiting to fly, and Salomeh held her breath.

Through the open door behind him, she could see many others craning their necks to see what he would do to her.

His eyes searched everywhere. His gaze rose to hers. She dared a glance outside again. His gaze followed hers over his shoulder, he grunted, and let his fist fly.

Salomeh screamed.

The blow grazed her as she smashed into a basket of his belongings behind her. She sprawled across the ground crying.

Laughter tumbled through the door before she heard it bang closed. She looked up, and he squatted in front of her, his eyes narrow and hard.

She pushed to sit up.

His brows pulled together until they almost touched, and he sighed several times. There was something he wanted to know, but there was no way to ask anything of one another. They spent so little time together since she'd arrived here, and they knew little more than each other's names and how to communicate yes and no. At last he pointed a finger at her, nearly poking her in the hollow of her throat. He thrust his finger at the door with his brows arched high.

Salomeh shook her head furiously and showed him one of his shirts she had mended. she pointed at wool she had pulled from the sheep and started to spin on a crude spindle she had fashioned out of a fat stumpy branch pulled from the wall. Finally, she showed him the leather and the rock she had used to continue his work of scraping it clean. She held out her trembling palms showing the many cuts her efforts had caused. She pointed to herself, "Salomeh," and patted the floor, "here."

Volkard's shoulders slipped down as a long slow breath seeped from him. He dropped to his knees and his head hung.

She cleared her throat and tipped her head toward the wall where light peaked through and mimicked looking through the holes.

He sprang to his feet so fast Salomeh jumped. His hard steps on the packed earth vibrated beneath her as he paced.

What was going on? Her stomach rolled. Gooseflesh rose on

her skin.

Volkard burst from the hut with a roar, and the unseen spies scampered away. Something thumped against the wall, and the light coming through the holes vanished. He stormed back in like a twisting wind coming off the Mediterranean. A string of angry words raced over his lips.

Salomeh swallowed her fear. The evening meal would not be for hours yet, but those outside would be waiting to see her swollen face. She stood, her movement stopping his renewed pacing. Taking his hand, she formed it into a fist and bumped her cheek with it.

He jerked from her grasp, stepped back, and shook his head.

Once again, Salomeh put her own fist against her face while closing the distance between them. He still refused. She swiped her finger through a dark patch of mud at the edge of the wall and smeared it along her jaw and pointed outside. "They have to see the damage," the words came out of her mouth though he wouldn't understand.

He backed from her until he bumped into the side of his hut. "Nein!" The sharp word was punctuated by a stiff shake of his head.

She turned, moving toward the opposite wall. Finding a chunk of wood, she smashed it into her mouth, and bit down on her lip to stifle the yelp.

Volkard spun her around and slapped the log from her hands. He cradled her face as he turned it this way and that to see the extent of the injury. He still held her face with both hands as he stooped to look directly in her eyes. "Nein," he said again. His thumbs caressed her cheeks.

She lowered her gaze, pointed at the door, and said, "Etiam—yes." It had to be done so they wouldn't suspect him.

By the time supper came, the holes in his wall were patched and her lip was split and swollen. Few people milled about outside. As Volkard led her to the fire, she trembled. An itching sensation prickled across her skin. She fought for breath. "Christus," she whispered.

CHAPTER

NINE

Volkard was ripped from her side before they made it three steps out the door. He roared and grunted. Flesh hit flesh.

She turned. Two men held Volkard to the ground beating him. Two others advanced on her—one was the man from the river. Salomeh spun and ran. A wall of women stood shoulder-to-shoulder in her path. She swerved back toward the hut. The door slammed in front of her. Unable to find safety, she was knocked face-first to the ground, air fled from her lungs, and bursts of light danced in her vision.

A hand jammed under her stomach, seized the front of her tunic, and flipped her to her back. The man from the river sat on top of her. Gripping the two ends of the tear Volkard had started, he tore her tunic completely open.

Air flooded her lungs, and she released it in a terrified scream. Scratching at his face she tried to break free.

The roar of a wild animal rent the night air.

Her wrists were snatched and held down above her head by another man, leaving the one atop her free to do as he pleased.

The roar called out again and another struggle sounded. Something crashed and a howl of pain added its chord to the decadent melody.

Salomeh screamed again. She thrashed, twisting in the firm hold. A bone snapped and bolts of pain shot through her hand. Raising her legs, she tried to kick the man in the back with her knees.

He flipped his feet over her legs stopping her distraction.

She shrieked again. "Christus, save me!"

A hand reverberated against her face adding stinging pain to the throbbing. As the aching waves lapped at the skin on her face, a hand closed around her throat. She fought for breath.

Her attacker muttered something, as the world spun and darkened. He shifted his weight and something pierced her side.

A cry of pain squeezed passed his hand.

Bellowed words and another roar distracted her assailant. He never had time to turn around. The tip of a sword burst through the evil man atop her, spraying her with his blood. The blade disappeared, and he crumpled to the ground beside her bringing Volkard into view. His blade rose again to strike at the other man holding her arms.

The man released her and crawled back away from the enraged blond warrior.

Volkard bellowed, his sword—dripping with blood—held high above his head.

Coughing, Salomeh gathered up the ends of her tattered garment covering herself as she rolled on her side inched toward him.

Volkard, roared. Words spewed from his lips in a long raging string. He stepped over Salomeh pointed the tip of his blade those standing around, and thrust it toward them. He stepped back, grabbed her by the arm, and jerked her to her feet. While he still kept the others at bay, his free arm encircled her waist, and he tossed her over his shoulder.

She whimpered at his roughness and her injuries.

He backed toward his hut, kicked open the door, and they disappeared inside.

He stood her on the floor, as she held her hand against her body. He secured the door, snatched up one of his shirts, handed it to her, and turned his back.

She moved to the back of the hut but gasped as she tried to remove her ruined garment. She pressed the tail of the rent tunic against the flowing blood. Her entire body trembled, and the sight of the scratches across her started her sobbing. The deep cries shot spasms of pain through her side. She dropped to her knees and braced her arm tight to her against the agony.

"Salomeh?" Volkard's gentle voice called her from the tortorus storm. He knelt beside her, but his light touch made her flinch, and she pulled away with a yelp. "Salomeh," he whispered again, more tender, more pleading. His hand touched the top of her head, but the sobs only increased.

His hand slid with slow tenderness until it rested on her shoulder.

She did not pull from him.

His hand travelled farther and she winced as he brushed the site of her injury. "Salomeh?" He held the hem of the shirt that she pressed to the wound and inched it up.

A cry caught in her throat, and she bit down on her lower lip.

One hand caressed her arm. "Salomeh." He replaced the cloth and had her return the pressure as more words followed. Though she didn't understand, the tone whispering them spoke of kindness, tenderness, and safety.

He stood, startling her. He tossed aside garments until he held a torn pair of braccae in his hands. He rent them further, separating leg from leg, and then pulled each apart from top to bottom. With four long lengths of fabric, he gathered more items and came to kneel beside her again. His eyes searched her face. He laid the strips over her lap and raised a threaded needle for her to see. In his other hand, he reached a slender stick to her mouth.

She clamped her lips closed and shook her head.

He placed it between his teeth and bit down on it, then offered it to her again.

Still she refused. He left it there, his gaze imploring her to take it. "Salomeh," he whispered. She sighed and opened her mouth.

He helped her lay on her side so he could access her injury. Again is unwavering gaze locked with hers. He gave a single slow nod. She held her breath as she slightly bobbed her head.

The needle pierced her skin, and she shrieked sending the stick tumbling.

He held her quaking body still for several minutes as she fought for an even breath. He finished the stitching as she cried. Next, he smeared the area with the ointment he'd used on her feet and legs, then folded one of the strips of cloth, covered the wound with it, and wrapped another snuggly around her securing the first in place. It was hard to breathe and the injury throbbed, but she managed to don the clean shirt he'd offered her earlier.

Next, he reached his hands out for hers.

Quivering, she relinquished them.

As before, his warm and supple fingers explored for injuries. He inclined his head, moving her hands back to her lap. He walked the length of his home searching all his chests and baskets, collecting bits here and there. Scanning the walls, he pulled out another stick before returning to sit before her. He took her hand again and placed a fat twig below the third finger of her left hand. Seeming to be pleased with its size, he set it aside and brought the first stick to her lips again.

Once she bit down on it, he gripped her her injured digit, again staring at her and gave a single nod.

She inclined her head slowly.

He pulled against his hand that held her wrist until the bone was aligned again.

She moaned around the wood in her mouth. Tears ran down her face.

He placed the branch under her finger and wrapped it with another slender piece of one of the remaining strips.

She let the bit of wood in her mouth drop and tried to stifle her cries.

He rose again and went to the jug on the table near the door only to return a few minutes later with a cup of beer. He placed his hand on her face, pain nearly as deep as her own etched on his features. He lifted the drink to her lips, and she tasted the bite of the healing herbs.

She emptied the cup and felt the dizziness take hold. Volkard covered her with an animal skin. His hand cradled her face.

They had to leave here. Soon. How could she tell him?

He stroked her face, humming softly as the most recent horrors faded and exhaustion and the tonic pulled her towards sleep's abyss.

A hand clamped over her mouth, jerking her from the oblivion of slumber.

"Salomeh?" A harsh whisper filled the darkness.

She used her good hand to try and pry away the obstruction.

"Salomeh. Volkard." He lowered his face though it was still covered in shadows. "Salomeh, shhhh," he soothed.

She relaxed under his grasp and nodded against his hand.

The hand eased from her face and, after a time, she felt it trail down her arm until his fingers laced with hers. While his other hand supported her back, he eased her to her feet. He waited until she steadied and then released her.

She could hear him moving around but couldn't tell what he was doing. At one point he bumped into her. She yelped out of surprise more than pain.

Moments passed before his hand found hers again and their fingers entwined, he led her through the animal pen. No sheep sounded, the cow didn't brush against her—the animals were gone. They left his hut through the animal door and stepped into the waning moonlight.

CHAPTER

TEN

Volkard had been pushing Salomeh too hard. She'd had no time to really rest after the attack, but he needed to get to somewhere safe. She never would be with him. Her pace had slowed considerably in the last hour. He stopped again, and it took no encouagment from him for her to lean against a tree gasping.

He moved a little way farther to a small rise, crouched, closed his eyes, and listened. Did they follow yet? He heard nothing, but he knew many skilled warriors filled Kordt's tribe. If they followed, he would learn of it too late. He never should have joined Kordt's murderous band, but he'd been left with few options. He turned to glance back at Salomeh—there were even less now.

The holy woman's tangled hair, the color of oiled leather, lay jumbled around her small oval face. Her head tipped back against the tree, and her mouth hung slightly open as she still fought to breathe. Pain etched deep into her features. She needed rest, time to heal. They couldn't spare even a moment. He was only grateful the injury to her side had only been a shallow slash and not a deep thrust. Most did not heal from such a penetrating wound to the gut.

Volkard again looked out over the land shrouded in deep shadows. He could leave her now. Now—later—did it matter? He saved her at the villa, but the holy woman would never be safe as long as he was near.

Volkard stood, stretching his back before hefting the pack back onto his shoulders. If he could manage it without hurting her, he would carry her too. Every possession he could gather now dragged at his shoulders. This was all he had to call his own in the world. He had again lost a home—in truth it was little more than a hovel, but it had been his.

Enough of this misery. Action. Do something! He stomped back down the rise.

Volkard moved toward her. Go? Stay? Were his small flock and cow still hidden? Had Kordt taken them? Or wild animals devoured them? Get the woman back to her people, retrieve the livestock, and find an isolated place to live out your days, Vol. It is the best you can hope for.

Snap!

Volkard turned to stone, his hand on the hilt of his sword.

Salomeh never stirred.

Snap! Pop!

He held his breath. Kordt's men would never be so careless.

A mountain goat wandered out of the trees and walked between him and Salomeh. It didn't seem to notice them as it ambled off into the trees again.

His shoulders fell and a long slow breath evaporated from him collapsing him further. He approached her, but she didn't respond. "Salomeh?"

Nothing.

He touched her arm, and she tilted into him. He caught her small frame before she fell, but she startled awake and yelped. He jumped as well. His heart fluttered for a few beats before he pushed her back toward the tree.

Her head lulled back and her eyes drooped.

"Salomeh."

She propped one eye open with some effort. The poor woman was beyond exhaustion.

He waved her forward and started to walk. By the third step, she had not moved to follow, so he called her name again. She lifted her head, but still didn't leave the support of the tree. He stopped and said her name again followed by a muttered curse he was grateful the righteous one couldn't understand.

She pushed away from the tree and staggered forward, a whisper fluttering over the fine line of her lips in response.

He doubted whatever the holy woman uttered had been vulgar, but it was clear she did not wish to comply. He looped his arm in hers and her head rested just below his shoulder as her weak grasp clung to him. They continued north.

The deep night turned into pre-dawn light as Volkard again hoped Kordt sent his men in pursuit to the south. It would make more sense to head to the nearest Roman occupied area and return the woman, but Volkard wouldn't make it so easy for them to find her—and kill him.

Volkard rolled his shoulders and stretched his back. He had seen enough of death. He no longer wanted to be a man of the sword. He could live a thousand years and never take another life or witness the untimely death of an innocent. He glanced down on the top of Salomeh's head. As soon as the holy one was safe.

Her feet scraped over the ground. She stumbled.

Volkard's nerves vibrated. They shouldn't stop, but he feared she couldn't continue. He wrapped a steadying arm around her, careful not to injure her as he provided more support. "By Oden's beard, for you, Salomeh, I would kill again. For you, I will die."

CHAPTER

ELEVEN

As the sun warmed the sky, a dwelling came into view in the distance. Volkard steered Salomeh toward it as he supported more of her slight weight with each step.

"Christus," she whispered again. She had called out to her God throughout the night and now come morning, she still managed to place one foot in front of the other.

The structure was lost behind a hill for a time. Volkard walked them around the base of the rise saving her the climb. As the dwelling came back into view, Volkard groaned.

The back corner of the roof had caved in. Weeds grew over the steps and the door had fallen away. No one had lived here for some time, and he now wasn't even sure it was Roman. He couldn't find aid for her here. But perhaps with the gods' help, he could find her a proper Roman garment and allow her a short rest.

Volkard stopped a couple of paces from the entrance and released Salomeh. She whimpered and reached for him swaying with the effort. He removed her hand, put it at her side, and turned to walk away. She followed. He placed his hand on her shoulders and held her still, shaking his head. As he released her, she wavered. Truly it was a wonder the woman was still standing.

He moved a few feet away, but turned to see Salomeh still followed. "Nein," he said stopping her once again. He needed to assure the place was safe—but he had no way to make her understand.

She lifted her head until their gazes met. Her lovely brown eyes, that reminded him of the rich soil of his homeland, were drenched in tears.

Volkard stepped from her and drew his sword. "I go to make sure all is safe, then you come."

She searched his face. He knew she didn't understand but hoped talking would calm her. Her head drooped, and she stilled.

He slipped inside the old home. Insects and dead leaves were the only things making their home here now. The remnants of a broken chair lay in the first room. The other chambers held little else. He found one room, near the back with no openings to the outside. It had an ample view of the center of the dwelling, and the cell next to it had a gaping hole in the wall. It would serve his purpose for shelter and yet allow easy escape should they need to flee.

Volkard dropped his pack. A rat scurried over his boot and out of the room. He exited the house through the hole and surveyed the surroundings. If they needed to run, he would take her west. The trees stood nearest to the house there. A rocky outcropping, twice the height of a man, lay in that direction also. One would provide them good cover and the other high ground if he needed to defend their position.

Assured he could keep the holy woman safe, he walked back toward the front of the house. Salomeh was not where he had left her. She wasn't near the entrance or back along the trail. "Salomeh." No reply answered. He raced to the top of the hill they had come around to get a better view of the surrounding land. Nothing. He tried to track her starting where he'd left her.

He found a smaller boot impression near his own headed to the house. He raced to the opening and burst through the open doorway. "Salomeh?" He searched every room calling her name but saw no more than he had on the first inspection.

He came back toward the entrance to return to the last boot impression. Rounding the corner he spotted her—slumped against the wall in a deep depression to the right of the doorway.

Volkard leaned forward bracing his hands on his knees. His heart thundered in his ears. His breath surged from him. Fear like this had not gripped him since he was a child—the night his mother died in his arms.

He stamped his foot and ground his teeth trying to shake the hold Salomeh had on him. After all, she meant nothing to him. A victim. One he was compelled to save though it cost him everything. No more than necessity bound them together. He cursed, for he couldn't even convince himself of the blatant lie. So why then couldn't he leave her and go? She needed him.

His breathing calmed, and his heartbeat settled. He stared. Did she breathe? His heart fluttered. What about this woman stirred him so? Sure, she was a female, and it had been long since he had lain with a woman. But Salomeh's pull on him was different.

He approached her. "Salomeh?"

Nothing.

He touched her arm.

Still she didn't move.

He brushed her face and lifted her chin.

She whimpered.

Volkard released the breath captured and held in his chest. Salomeh still lived, and strangely, his soul rejoiced. He scooped her into his arms and moved her to the room where he had left his pack. He knelt and settled her in the cleanest spot—near the door but tucked out of sight against the wall. As he pulled from her, she took hold of his shirt.

He pried her fingers free.

She seized his shirt in a different spot. "Volkard," she cried.

His stomach clenched. His heart flipped. His name on her lips, whispered from such need, bound him to her. It reawakened deep desires within him.

He tried again to escape, but she would not allow him. Clinging, she laid her head on his chest refusing to release him or be released by him.

The warmth of her triggered a more primal need. Did the woman not understand what she did to him? He could not remain here. With her snuggled in his arms, he would not be able to stop himself from taking advantage of her, hurting her spirit and body —thus damning his own soul. He waited for her to quiet—to relax against him—before he slipped from her grasp and walked the perimeter trying to rid himself of the emotions and desires she woke in him.

Salomeh, the Roman, the woman touched by the gods, would be the end of him.

But he wasn't sure he cared.

CHAPTER

TWELVE

Volkard rolled his shoulders and secured his bow across his back. As the sun slipped toward the western horizon, he entered the dilapidated house. Once again, Salomeh was not in the place where he'd left her. Turning, he noticed her smaller boot prints mixed in with those he'd made in his search of the dwelling earlier in the morning. He shouldn't have left her alone.

The prints switched back over themselves as she too apparently went to every room. Volkard followed them in and out of every open space, back to the door, to the room with the hole in the wall, and back again. Salomeh was nowhere to be found.

"Salomeh." But she did not answer. He returned to the prints wandering in the carpet of dust. Another circuit, yet his search only served to destroy all evidence of either of them.

He reached out a hand on one wall to steady himself. His heart beat a furious pace booming in his ears. No other prints were inside but theirs. Her footsteps did not go near the outer door or the opening in the wall. He fought to calm his frantic breathing and his raging thoughts. "By the gods, I could not have saved her from so many only to lose her in an abandoned house," he growled to the emptiness. He threw his fist into the opposite wall with a roar.

Dirt showered down on him from the crumpling roof.

A stifled yelp floated to him from deeper inside the structure.

The only room he hadn't search was the one buried in rubble. Surely she hasn't… He spotted a single print of the toe of her boot a few inches inside the room and a good foot or more from where her last step had been. She had leapt from the main hall into the room leaving almost no evidence. Smart woman. Everything she did only endeared her to him all the more.

He moved toward the opening and crouched down to peer under a fallen beam. Deep shadows were all he saw, but he allowed his eyes time to adjust. Fur… fur with boots. She lay curled under the debris wrapped in the fur he had draped over her before they left. Only the soles of her boots were visible under the skin she clung tight about her.

"Salomeh?"

She didn't move.

He reached in and touched her foot.

She jerked away stirring the dust, which hid the musty odor of the rotting leaves for a few moments.

Volkard sneezed. He lay on his belly, thrust both hands in, grasped her ankles and yanked her out into the open space with him. "Salomeh!"

He moved to his knees and grasped the fur to remove it.

Her fists thrust out smacking him in the chest. She cried out and snatched her wounded hand back to cradle it against her ribs.

Salomeh's hair was usually the color of the rick dark bark on the trees of his home. Now it was littered with dust and bits of the roof timbers she had hidden under. Volkard brushed it from her face. Clean streaks in the dirt on her cheeks showed where her tears had flowed.

She slapped his hand away and struggled to sit up.

He tried to help her, but she continued to rebuff him. He stood, left her, and returned a moment later holding the pair of hares by the hind feet he trapped for their dinner.

She looked, then buried her face in her hands.

As Volkard worked to skin and dress the meat, her sniffles battered his heart. He should not have left her alone. But truth was he did plan to abandon her. It was his entire purpose for taking her from Kordt's village. Find a Roman village and leave her there. His resolve weakened at seeing her distress at having left her for mere hours.

His gaze drifted out the hole in the wall. They had yet to find any settlements—Roman or otherwise. Perhaps he took them too far north. They should move west as soon as the sun set.

Volkard jerked back his hand as flames bit at his flesh. The small fire he started in the large room near the door had grown faster than he planned. He checked the red splash across the side of his hand. No deep damage. He set the meat over the flames and went back to Salomeh.

She sat with her head tipped back against the wall and one leg out straight in front of her. Her eyes were closed, but her brows where drawn together, and her lower lip sat clamped between her teeth.

He knelt beside her. "Salomeh," he whispered.

She turned her head away from him.

Volkard snatched hold of her chin and turned it back toward him. A flash of anger burst from him and he growled her name.

She opened her eye and shrank from him. Trembling in his harsh grasp, she stared. As he moved away she flinched.

Oh, if this woman wasn't infuriating. He clamped his jaw together, and using slow, gentle movements, he checked her finger and her side. Her crawling into the hiding place and his rough extraction had been poor choices on both their parts.

She cried as he touched her side.

He untied the bandages, applied more ointment he retrieved from his pack, and rewrapped the wound. She'd pulled a couple of his stitches, but the cut would heal in time. He left her and brought back some of the meat.

She refused it.

He tore off a piece and brought it to her lips.

She turned from him shaking her head.

He laid his other hand on her cheek and whispered her name. Their gaze held.

"Please," he whispered offering the tidbit again.

After a moment, she ate it.

He managed to get her to eat a little more before she refused again. He turned to move away, and she reached for him. As he turned back, she snatched her hand away and covered herself in the skin. But it didn't hide her trembling. He tried to explain with his hand motions he would be back, but she closed her eye as tears again wet her cheeks.

After covering the fire with dirt, checking the outside for Kordt's men, and securing the front door as best as he could, he returned to her. He sat beside her, and wrapping her in one arm, and pulled her to rest against him.

She melted into him and was asleep in moments.

Hours. Let her sleep for a few hours. He watched the shadows grow long out the hole in the wall. The holy woman warming his flesh pulled his thought from the plans of their escape. By Oden's beard, he needed to get away from this woman touched by the gods before he tainted her. But would he be able to walk away when the time came?

CHAPTER

THIRTEEN

Two days of trudging over the root covered ground and weaving among the trees at last brought them to the outskirts of a Roman town. Volkard led her inside a raided villa, much like the one he had saved her from. The marble and tile rooms were laid out in similar fashion and he came to a room like the one he had found her in. He recalled the image of first seeing her kneeling in prayer to the One she called Christus, and it made his heart skip as it had that day.

Volkard shook off the memory and moved through the structure. Searching the remains. he couldn't find a tunic like she wore before, only a woman's long garment. He offered it to Salomeh, but she shook her head.

Volkard took her by the hand and led her out the front door. Pressing the garment into her palm he forced her fingers to close around it and held it there. Using his other hand, he pointed to the town. "Time for you to go back."

Salomeh pulled from his hold, left the dress with him, and re-entered the house. She disappeared for a time before returning with several garments of her own. She held them up before him judging the size. A man's toga, that was entirely too short, a tunic that was too narrow, followed by a couple of others before she held up a servant's tunic very similar to the one she had worn.

"So, I am to be your slave now?" he grumbled. He also shook his head.

She took the lady's garment from him and pressed the tunic into his chest, her brows raised.

He gave a sharp jerk of his head and stepped back, allowing the hateful thing to drop to the steps. "I will be slave to no man—or woman."

Moving slow and minding her injury, she reached down and collected the tunic. Wadding both garments in her hands, she stomped to the charred remains of the victims of the villa. Her uninjured hand rose over her head.

Volkard grabbed her by the wrist before she could destroy what white remained of the linen, making either unwearable. He took them from her and offered her the woman's dress again.

She spun on her heel and moved deeper into the villa.

"Salomeh!" he bellowed, threw the garments against the wall, and stomped outside. He snatched up his pack and walked away. He found a vantage point where he had a view of the ruins. He crouched and watched, waiting for her to leave.

Hours passed. The sun touched the horizon, and still she didn't leave to go to the town. She didn't come looking for him either. Volkard growled and thrust his dagger into the soil beside where he sat.

"Go back to your people, woman. What are you waiting for? I have to get back to my animals." He grumbled into the growing darkness, knowing his tiny flock was already either dead or taken by Kordt's people. He admitted to himself he would not be going back the way they came.

He stood. "Fine, I have done for you what I can. Your Christus watch over you now. I must find a new life for myself." Surely, there is somewhere men do not war. Somewhere I can live in peace.

As he turned, movement caught his eye. Creeping out of the shadows toward the villa, six dark figures moved in silence.

He dropped his pack, snatched up his dagger, and raced to intercept them. His heart nearly seized in his chest for in only a matter of steps he realized, too late, they would reach her first. A warning call strangled in his throat—it would alert the attackers as fast as signal Salomeh.

He sped across the uneven earth recklessly. If anything happens to the holy woman because of me… His stomach knotted, nearly doubling him in pain at the thought of what they would do to her. *Thor, save—No, Christus—save Your holy one,* his heart cried.

CHAPTER

FOURTEEN

Dagger in one hand, sword in the other, Volkard vaulted up the steps. The attackers were already inside, out of sight, as he flew through the door. Looping his arm over the first's head, Volkard drew the smaller weapon across the man's throat dropping him to the tile before the man had time to turn. The second man came into the room from a side chamber. Volkard ran him through with the longer blade before he could release a cry.

The blood lust upon him, Volkard also pulled his blade across the dead man's throat. Heat surged through his limbs and heart in slow massive bursts echoing in his ears. The blood. Bright. Flowing. Pooling. More. Like the hunger of a slave who had not been offered food in a week, Volkard needed to spill more blood. He hunched down on one knee. He stilled his breathing, listening for the movement of his next target.

The next two appeared farther down the central marble passageway from opposite sides at the same time. "Nothing," one said to the other.

"We know she is here. We tracked her."

Volkard recognized their voices. Kordt's men. One, Aiko, was the man who'd held Salomeh's hands as the other attacked her.

"But she didn't go out."

"I will have that Roman whore…"

Volkard inched toward them, keeping against the wall. He sprang from the shadows. Rage and death consumed him as his sword came down on the first relieving him of his head. It dropped at the other's feet staring up at him with blank eyes.

Wasting no time, Volkard thrust his dagger at Aiko, as he swung his sword around at him too. Their swords rang out as they collided. "Volkard, you son of a dog. We thought you had at last abandoned your toy."

"You will not lay your filthy hands on her," Volkard vowed and to make his words true, he spun and brought his sword down, removing the man's left hand.

Aiko howled.

Volkard's pulse thundered in his ears, the blood squirting from the arm making him euphoric. He drew his sword tip down the injured man's right arm, opening it to leak the precious red liquid. His heart beat harder as he dug his weapon's point into the man's thigh.

The man dropped smiling up at Volkard, "I may not get the pleasure, but surely Kurnt, and Gregor have found her by now. The two of them—"

Volkard slashed out with his dagger slitting the man's throat and silencing him for good. A tremor of panic shook Volkard as he fought to reign in the blood lust. He had to find her before they —he could not finish the thought.

Fire burst across his shoulder, and he whirled to block the next blow. "Gregor."

"Ungrateful whelp. We took you in, gave you a home, an honored place among us, a share of the Roman spoils. And you turn on us."

"A home among you? Yet no woman to call my own. Spoils! Only those left over after you've all taken your share. Honored place among you? Thor's hammer! I have been little more than dung on your boot since I arrived. And had I not bested three of Kordt's men with my sword, I wouldn't have lived to find even that small place."

Gregor laughed, circling him. "You never crossed blades with me, dung."

The blades rang out in several matched attacks. The noise reverberated off the marble surfaces and echoed in Volkard's ears. Gregor worked to maneuver him against a wall. Volkard spun from the blade thrust letting it clang against the surface.

Volkard turned and backed a few feet away into the center of the room.

Gregor charged at him.

Seizing Gregor by the wrists as he came, Volkard fell to his back and flipped Gregor over his head. Gregor landed with a thud, clattering the broken tiles, and groaned. Leaping to his feet, Volkard drove his sword down toward Gregor's chest, but only caught his arm as the man rolled away. Volkard's feet were kicked out from under him, and he found himself on his back looking up at Gregor's approaching blade tip.

Volkard slapped the descending deathblow with his sword and pulled Gregor down toward him. Under complete control of the blood lust now, Volkard could barely wait until Gregor was within dagger reach. He thrust his short blade up into Gregor's ribs. "Consider our blades crossed." Volkard gave the blade a twist with a growl as he threw off the dying man. Volkard pushed to his feet and thrust his sword into Gregor's chest and watched the last pumps of the man's heart force out his blood with a gurgle.

The blood called to him, but the smirk left on Gregor's lifeless face reminded him of Kurnt and the danger to Salomeh.

Volkard left the dead and raced up the stairs. He found them. Salomeh lay still, her arms out at her sides. Volkard staggered banging into the doorframe. *I can't be too late.*

Kurnt's back faced him as Volkard entered the door. Kurnt yanked the last of Salomeh's clothing from her body. Her gaze locked with Volkard's. Her glare accused him. Kurnt lifted off her to release his personal weapon, Volkard surged forward and thrust his blade into the man's back.

Kurnt bellowed and pulled his own blade, slashing out—but not at Volkard—at Salomeh.

Volkard whirled in front of him and blocked the first erratic slash and kicked Kurnt onto his back. He slapped the man's blade away with his own. He thrust his sword into one of Kurnt's thighs, then the other. Volkard's breaths burst from his lungs as he stomped after Kurnt who attempted to crawl away. He cut away the hand holding the sword Kurnt had hoped to use on Salomeh. Again, pleasure stirred in Volkard until he was near giddy. He stabbed, poked, and cut the man long after he was dead. Only as a gasped breath scraped through the air, did Volkard turn his attention back to Salomeh.

She lay bare over the mosaic tiles still staring at the door—and another lust all together gripped him. A need far too long unmet. He closed his eyes against the sight of her and staggered forward. He fought not to be like the man he had just killed. He picked up the skin she had been wrapped in and threw it over her body. He could not do a heinous act to her.

He pressed his forehead against the cool tiles. *Thor, help me.*

He summoned every ounce of his strength, dropped to his knees and moved toward her, crawling on his hands and knees.

Still she stared out at nothing.

He reached to touch her face. Her hair moved and he saw blood on the floor. Kurnt had smashed her head into the titles to quiet her. "Salomeh," he whispered tapping her face.

Her eyes blinked and came into focus. As if animated by the power of a god, she came to life and fought against him.

Volkard struggled to keep her flailing arms at bay. "Salomeh. Salomeh! Volkard."

She quieted and stared at him.

"Volkard," he said again.

Smack! Her hand smashed against his face and drove him back to his heels.

He blinked to clear his vision. Words flew from her lips, and though he knew they were spewed in anger, the Latin tongue made it sound more like singing.

She reached out and tried to strike him again. Her hand caught nothing but air. Her gaze shifted to the blood-covered dagger he had dropped on the floor. While she reached for it, Volkard slid another foot from her. But she didn't raise it toward him. She laid it across her wrist—but the splint on her finger hampered her grip.

Flipping it to her other hand she raised it up to plunge in her own middle.

"NIEN!" he screamed and lunged for the weapon. She cut his arm in their struggle, but he would not allow her to harm herself.

They grappled for a few moments until Volkard wrenched the blade from her hand tossing it across the room. He pressed her arms against her chest still covered in the animal skin. Wrapping his arms around her, he sat and pulled her tight against himself. He tucked her head beneath his chin and rocked her. "Nien, nien. Do not hurt yourself. They did not succeed. You are still holy. Touched only by your God." His need for her clamored in every ounce of his body. "Christus, help her. She calls on Your name. Comfort her now, Christus."

Salomeh quieted in his arms, and began to weep.

Stirred by an unfamiliar calming in his own being, he continued to pray to this God he didn't know. "Christus, be gracious to her. Help her—Your servant." His flesh quieted even more. The thirst for blood, and her, melted away to be replaced by a peace unlike anything his gods had ever given him.

Exhaustion crept around the edge of the quieting of his spirit. It pulled at him until he slumped to the floor, still cradling Salomeh in his arms.

CHAPTER

FIFTEEN

Salomeh's whimpers of pain jerked Volkard out of sleep again. He opened his eyes to gaze on her, but she continued sleeping. He checked on her frequently in between removing the dead, hunting, preparing the meat for him and a broth for her, and pacing the room endlessly. Salomeh's eyes fluttered open from time to time but never focused on him.

The moon shone through a window deprived of shutters. Salomeh started to move and cried out. He leapt to her side, whispering to her softly. He held a cup of tepid broth to her lips. She drank almost half before turning her head away.

He stood, stretched, and winced at the wound in his own back. He'd done his best to clean and dress the blade slash left in his flesh. Moving to the wall he pressed the wound against the cool marble and a sigh sagged him back into the steadfast surface.

Each day she remained awake a little longer, and he helped her eat more. After a week, Salomeh stirred beside him pulling Volkard from staring at the ceiling. The day was already half spent by the light coming through the window.

Salomeh clutched at the fur covering her and stared up at him.

Alert, her eyes took in more of her surroundings. If only they could speak to one another. Was she well?

She fought to sit up, whimpered, and bit her lip. He needed to check her wound, but he didn't dare in her current state of undress. Finally, after several more days, she sat steadily, fully herself once again. Color filled her cheeks and her stomach rumbled. He held her gaze a moment longer and made up his mind. He walked from the room, the soft pad of his boots whispered across the hall to a chamber next door. He shed his familiar clothing and returned to Salomeh moments later dressed in a Roman slave tunic. Volkard held the woman's garment out to her.

A hand appeared between the folds of animal skin, but she didn't take the dress from him. She mimicked scrubbing her dirty arm. He turned, the clap of the Roman sandals against the marble floor echoed as he bound down the stairs. Scooping up a chipped earthenware bowl, he dashed out to the stream trickling near the house. The leather sandal straps pinched his calves as he crouched to fill the vessel with water. Bits of grass caught between his toes and the sandal. "Useless, impractical, idiotic footwear. And the Romans think themselves civilized. Boots! By Thor's hammer, what was wrong with boots?" He stomped back into the villa and up the stairs, placed the bowl and a bit of cloth near Salomeh and prepared to leave. A pebble lodged in his sandal, he cursed.

Salomeh glanced down at the tiny vessel and smirked. She slipped one grimy foot out from the fur and then the other which appeared dirtier than the first. Volkard considered the scant amount of water he had provided her. He nodded, put the bowl on her lap, and scooped her up into his arms. She was light, frail almost. But he knew better. She survived a brutal attack by a man twice her size. Stubbing his toe on a chunk of fallen wall, he cursed again as he carried her down the disheveled steps. Volkard sat her on the edge of a low tiled wall. It formed a square in the middle of the room. He had seen one like it filled with water in the villa where he saved Salomeh.

He made sure she wouldn't fall, brushed the leaves and debris into one corner, and scooped it out. After numerous trips to the streams he added enough water for her to clean herself. He looked at her questioningly. She nodded. Volkard laid the Roman gown on the ledge opposite her and turned leaving her to wash in private.

He waited outside and did not see her for some time. What if she needed help? What could he do? Perhaps he should go in and check on her. Volkard paced with indecision.

At last she emerged from the house, dressed in a long almost white linen tunic with a wide blue sash draped over her left shoulder and tied around her slim waist. Her dark hair was brushed. There had been many bits and pieces of belongings left about in the house, she must have found the items she needed among them. Her hair lay smooth and flowed from the crown of her perfect head, over her exquisite shoulders, and down to her shapely waist.

She hobbled to him watching him with wide eyes. Her gaze searched his face. He raised his hand, slowly as not to frighten her, and cradled her cheek.

He caressed her skin with his thumb, gazed into her eyes, and again his heart set its course. "I will not leave you again. Until death calls to one of us, I will be where you are, and you will be safe. This I vow." The issued oath settled within him: the peace returned as from the evening he prayed over her. The peace he first learned of when he spoke the name of her God.

She tipped her head, brows drawn together.

He reached out his hand to her.

She looked at it for a moment and placed hers in his. His hand engulfed her small one. Smooth to his rough, and a dark honey in color to his pale young wheat. But it fit. Nestled there in his palm —filling it with warmth. All the gods help him, but this woman, he could not even speak to had captured his heart.

He turned to lead her from the house of death, but she pulled from him. He turned to her confused.

A slim smile peeked across her lips, as she held up sections of her hair that framed her face. She pulled them back, with a wince, to the crown of her head.

He stared at it, until she drew a circle around it with her finger and acted as though she tied it.

Volkard took his dagger and cut a bit of the leather lacing from one of his hated sandals. He handed her the piece.

She secured the tie around the hair she held from her temples to keep it out of her face, but left the rest fall down her back. Now she looked like the wealthy Roman women he had seen—and killed—before.

Next, she started to bend over but yelped in pain. Holding her side, she straightened and tried to take a deep breath.

Volkard raised his hand to examine her, but she waved him off shaking her head. Her gaze shifted to her feet and she pulled up the hem of her garment, revealing an unbound sandal she had found for herself.

Volkard knelt, placed her foot atop his thigh, and secured the strap up her shin. He did the same with the other, her hand resting on his shoulder for balance. Touching her flesh, feeling her fingers against him, he felt the warmth rise in him again. The job done, he popped to his feet and raked his hands over his face to brush aside the feelings assailing him.

She straightened her garment and turned raising a questioning brow to him.

He doubted the woman had any idea the effect she had upon him. He gave her a curt nod, flung his pack over his uninjured shoulder, and led the way from the house—and toward the town. All their gods help them, but he knew there was as much danger for them in the Roman town as among the tribes. How would he save her against so many?

CHAPTER

SIXTEEN

"Volkard," she huffed his name stopping his forward march. She leaned against a tree clutching at her side and panting.

He pointed to the city just beyond the tree line. It wasn't much farther.

She held up her hand until her breathing calmed. She pushed off the tree, and he turned to start walking. "Volkard."

He turned raising his arms in frustration. If he had to play the slave, could they not be about it?

She put up her hands and walked toward him. Pulling the pack from his shoulder, she sat it on the ground with a small gasp and covered it with leaves.

He snatched it up again, shaking his head.

She took hold of his arm and pointed to the Roman citizens they could see walking the streets. None carried packs. Cloth wrapped bundles perhaps slung over a shoulder, but no packs.

Next, she pointed to his sword and dagger, shaking her head.

Volkard stepped from her, "Nien!" There would be no way to protect her without his weapons.

She crossed her arms and plopped down on the ground. Her eyes clenched closed, and she bit down on her lip. She'd landed too hard.

A just payment for being such an obstinate woman, he thought. He'd given up so much already. He would not relinquish the last of what he owned. He crossed his arms as well staring at her to relent.

Salomeh struggled to her feet, pointed at his sword and pack, then to the city and held her hands out before him as though they were bound.

He raised his head and again stared out to the city full of his enemy.

How did she make him understand? He was obviously a warrior. She was dressed in a noble woman's stola. If the Romans discovered the truth and caught her, they would start by whipping her and end by killing them both.

She had to make him understand. She moved his hands until they also appeared bound. Pointing to herself, she started making whipping motions. She acted out each strike to a flinch and a small cry.

Volkard stared at her, his eyes growing wider. The blue in them darkened.

She pointed at him, "Germani," and flipped out the garment covering her. "Stola."

He didn't understand.

Volkard had done so much to save her. Now they were entering a world she understood. It would now be her responsibility to protect him. She would not see him sold in the slave markets like she had been. Her heart couldn't bear the thought. But if he didn't cooperate, they would never make it to a place of real safety. *It does exist, doesn't it, Lord? Please, tell me there is a place for us out there. A place where we can live in peace—together.*

Volkard hadn't thought of the status implied when he found the bits of clothing. It was Roman. She needed to look like them and not like one of a German tribe, but she was a servant. The garment she wore was that of a noble woman. She was in danger if her people learned of her deception—and of course there was her German slave-man. They needed to not draw attention.

Again—for her—to save her—he relented. The pack and sword were hidden, but he would not part with the dagger. It was the last thing his father had given him.

She reached for it.

"Nein!"

She put up one hand in surrender, but the other still reached for the blade. She said something and after several moments of reluctance he placed it on her palm. She turned some and slipped the dagger under her sash along her back on the opposite side of her injury. She flounced the fabric, pulled at the layers of her sash until it covered the weapon, and looked up at him.

He nodded, though a scowl pulled at his lips.

She rubbed her fingers together questioning him. "Denari?"

Volkard crossed his arms again.

She held up a single finger.

He dug a small silver coin with some Roman emperor engraved upon it from a pouch hidden under his belt and placed it in her hand.

She turned, started walking, and he came along side. "Non." She placed her hands on his chest stopping him. She walked away from him backwards several steps, turned, and started forward again waving him to follow. While he tried to close the distance, she turned to him, and placed her hands on her hips. "Non." She shook her head. She put her palm out toward him stopping until she achieved the same distance between them and motioned him to begin again.

So, the dutiful slave walks a half pace behind. He nodded his understanding as she turned to glance at him.

As they neared the main street, he watched her straighten, square her shoulder, and raise her chin. Her walk took on one of authority. She strolled boldly down the street making servants and slaves step aside for her.

It was in this moment Salomeh completely captured his heart.

CHAPTER

SEVENTEEN

Volkard followed Salomeh's purposeful steps as she moved through the streets to the center of town. Carts clogged the streets keeping the two new arrivals on the sidewalks. Stalls with vendors hawking all manner of wares called out in their sing-song Latin tongue. Salomeh moved a stand where a woman sold cloth. She stopped for a moment feeling several pieces, but she was doing something more. In the dirt she drew an arc with the toe of her sandal. The merchant woman did not respond, and Salomeh moved on. She did the same at a stand with bread, bought a small loaf, and handed him half as they continued down the street. She paused at the stand of a lean man selling bobbles for her hair, but she didn't linger here either.

Volkard followed closer in the crowd, but few took notice of him. Every eye, both male and female, was drawn to Salomeh. Looking at her with all the other Romans in the market, he realized her skin and hair were warmer in color than most. From what part of the ever-encroaching Roman Empire had they captured her?

He rolled his shoulders and stamped down his desire to retrieve his dagger from her back and cut out every lustful, envious eye staring at her. *She is mine,* his heart growled.

Next, she moved to a vegetable stand. This time, while she drew the arc in the dust, the merchant looked all about, and drew an opposing arc crossing the two lines on one side and closing them on the other. It looked like a child's drawing of a fish.

As soon as Salomeh smiled at the woman, the merchant smeared their drawing as though she had never seen it. They talked over the woman's merchandise for a moment before Salomeh was led to the back of the stall. She turned to him before she disappeared and, as covertly as possible, waved for him to stay.

Volkard turned and looked at those mingling among the stalls. Most, like him, were dressed as slaves and servants. How could one country support so many in the lower and disadvantaged ranks? Romans—the more he knew of them, the more he hated them. His blood turned hot, surging through his body like fire. A toga-clad man, carried in a litter by four tunic-clad men, made his way through the market center. The rich man's progress caused the lowly people to scatter out of the way. Volkard seized a child by the collar and pulled him aside before he was trampled.

Volkard reached for his sword only to remember his hip was bare. His insides throbbed with his desire to see the fat Roman's blood spilled on the stones he rode over.

Something brushed his arm, and a hand squeezed his little finger. He turned, but no one stood beside him. The child had run off. No one even remained near him. He spotted Salomeh as she moved away through the crowd.

Volkard followed, trying not to allow much distance between them. She moved fast darting between people who walked much slower along the street. At cross streets, she paused for a moment, glanced down at a scrap in her hand, and continued in a new direction. More than once, he became distressed as he lost sight of her entirely as she rounded a corner.

They travelled through the densest part of the city and on through to the main road leading to and from the metropolis. Outside the town walls, the structures grew sparse until all disappeared. Salomeh turned back to him, a smile spread across her face. His heart fluttered. A woman's smile hadn't stirred him since his mother's. Or maybe a woman hadn't smiled at him in all these passing years. He dropped back allowing the distance to grow between them, just to clear his thoughts for a moment. She disappeared around a small bend in the road lined with trees, again causing a reaction in his feeble confused heart.

When Volkard rounded the corner, and spotted Salomeh approaching a building. His heart skipped a beat, and he ran to close the distance between them. She passed the rail out front to tie up horses and knocked on the door. A woman came out, and Salomeh spoke with her, again drawing the symbol in the dirt. The woman didn't close the figure but embraced Salomeh, kissing her on both cheeks.

Salomeh reached out her hand for him as he drew near, and he heard his name as she continued to talk with the woman.

The other woman stood about a hand taller than Salomeh, lighter hair plaited in one long strand down her back, and lighter skin—though neither were as light as his. She smiled at him, but it did not have the same effect on him as Salomeh's smile.

They were ushered into the dwelling where several tables and chairs greeted them in the first room.

The woman called out over her shoulder and a man appeared carrying cups. He placed them on a table where Salomeh took a seat and kissed the woman on the cheek. Introductions were made, and Volkard heard his name mentioned twice before the man disappeared.

Salomeh's hand fell over Volkard's forearm and tightened when he sat down beside her. Turning to her, he was surprised to see her radiating. A smile consumed her face and light danced in her eyes. She fidgeted. It seemed impossible for her to sit still.

Another man entered. A full head shorter than either woman, he had a narrow face with eyes set too close together. His entire face, from his drawn together brows to his puckish mouth, gave him a pinched look and reminded Volkard of a weasel.

The moment he drew near the table, his gaze fell on Salomeh. One corner of his mouth curved up, and his stare grew hungry. Muscles throughout Volkard's body clenched as he suppressed the deep desire to reach across the table and snap the man's neck.

A long string of Latin tumbled from Salomeh as the other woman left the room. The weasel turned toward him. He opened his mouth and flawless German flowed from him. Without inflection or life to the words, they fell flat between them.

"She asks, 'Why did you save me?'"

Her hand tightened on his arm, and Volkard turned to see her staring, not at the little man, but at him. This is what excited her so; they were about to communicate for the first time.

Volkard cleared his throat, glanced at the weasel who perhaps was not as bad as he first thought, and started speaking. After a few words, the little man started speaking to Salomeh, but she only looked at Volkard—as though no other was with them.

"I came to the villa to kill and loot as the chief of the village, Kordt, ordered. It happened the same as always. We broke in and killed all we found. They screamed and cried—begging for their lives, I assume. I entered the room where you took shelter and found several kneeling before the household idols—but not you. They wailed, waved me off, and tried to crawl away."

The radiance left her face. Tears pooled in her eyes. But she squeezed his arm and nodded.

"No matter the commotion around you, you never moved—not even flinched. You faced no statue or carving. You sat in the middle of the room and—though Tjaard swore he could not see it—I tell you, I saw you bathed in light from above. I felt it in my spirit. You could not be harmed. I knew then. You are a holy one, touched by the gods." He laid his hand over hers. "I wanted no more of killing and death, and I knew I would never find such a life if I killed you."

"Tjaard? He was the one you killed to save me?"

"There in the villa, yes. I tried to tell him what I saw—felt—believed—but he would not listen. His hatred of all things Roman would not allow him to hear me."

"And the others? They didn't wish you to save me either?"

He shook his head. He swallowed hard before he could find a way to utter the next words. "They wished me to… to take my pleasure… and then kill you. They did not understand why I insisted on bringing you with me."

"Why did you? It cost you everything."

He shook his head and searched the scratches in the table's top as though they might have some profound answer. "They could have returned to the villa and done to you as they have tried on several occasions since." His head shook again. "I had to make sure the favored one of the gods remained safe—and pure." Raising his head, he stared at her willing her to understand. "And I could not part from the stirring within me whenever you are near."

"But you left me. Abandoned me to return to your people."

He now tightened his hold on her. "They are not my people." He said with enough force to cause her to draw back from him by a degree. He took a breath and calmed himself. "I believed you would be safer with your people—away from me and the death that surrounds me."

"The Romans are not my people either," she said with a slim smile. "And you must have known, I have been safest with you, Volkard."

"Is that why you would not leave without me? Why you tried to hurt yourself rather than go on alone."

Her hand pulled from between his arm and his hand where it had rested, and she laid it on his cheek. "Christus spoke to me as well. I too feel the stirring of Him whenever you are near. I know God wants me to remain with you."

"Why would your gods want me to be with you?"

"God, only one. Christus—He loves you, Volkard."

"This Christus loves me?" Volkard's heart pounded in his chest and hammered in his ears—but whether it was from her touch or her words—he refused to say.

"Yes, Volkard. Christus loves you so much, He died for you."

"This God died—for me?"

The other woman abruptly. Urgent Latin words stopped their conversation. Salomeh stood and followed her. Since Volkard did not rise, still reeling from what she said, she reached for him and again talked to the little man.

"Romans are coming. You must hide," the weasel said still without any emotion. It made the hairs on the back of Volkard's neck stand on end. Truly, he did not like the diminutive man.

The woman pulled a rug from the floor the other man returned and opened a hatch hidden beneath. Salomeh turned and descended the ladder into the darkness below. With insistent waves of the woman's hand as she glanced toward the door, Volkard followed.

The hatch closed and the rug was replaced cutting off all light before he reached the bottom. "Salomeh?" he whispered.

A hand touched first his calf, then found his arm, as he stepped down carefully searching for each rung with his toe. She directed him down, laced her fingers in his, and led the way until his toe kicked something and she placed their hands on a stone seat. As soon as they were seated, she pressed herself against him until he wrapped his arm around her. Her head came to rest on his chest, and he could feel the rise and fall of her breathing against him. His body longed for hers, but his mind continually replayed her words. "Christus loves you. He died for you."

CHAPTER

EIGHTEEN

The clop of the soldiers' steps echoed off the floorboards overhead causing Salomeh to curl tighter into Volkard's embrace. The sound of nail-studded sandals rattled his nerves as well. He slid his hand down her back and retrieved the dagger she had hidden in the folds of her garment. With the dagger in his right hand and Salomeh tucked under his left arm, he strained to listen to the movements above.

The soldiers crossed the room above them. The clicking against the wood muffled as they moved farther back into the rooms beyond the first one. How many of them? Three? Four? He couldn't tell. The stomping came back directly above them, their sandals muted over the rug hiding their hatch. Three hard thumps sounded against the hatch.

Salomeh tensed against him.

Muttered voices filtered down through the boards. Three more stomps again sounded overhead, then farther away and once more in another place. Salomeh startled each time. She made no sound, but pressed herself against him until he struggled to move.

More footsteps were heard overhead moving toward the entrance as the sound grew fainter. The structure above became as silent as the room in the dark below. Salomeh relaxed. Her grip on his tunic held lessened. A long slow breath at last escaped her, and she melted against him.

They remained quiet in the dark. He sat the dagger on his thigh and leaned his head back against the wall. Again, her translated words came back to haunt him. "Christus loves you. He died for you."

The gods he knew cared little for humans—other than what lowly mortals could do for the immortals. For a foreign God he had never heard of to love him seemed, not only unlikely but, incomprehensible. And to further think that a God died and died *for* him? How did he make sense of things his mind could not fathom? Yet those incomprehensible notions stirred his heart— awakened his spirit—and filled him with peace.

The room flooded with light, causing Volkard to squeeze his eyes closed and grip both the dagger and Salomeh tighter.

"Salomeh, Volkard," the rest was unintelligible Latin.

Rising from his hold, she shielded her eyes with her injured hand and reached out for him with the other.

They climbed the ladder back into the inn. The woman handed them small cloth sacks and ushered them out the door. She embraced Salomeh, then both the woman and her man rested their hands on Salomeh and Volkard's heads. Bowing their heads, they spoke. He only understood his name and Salomeh's mentioned along with Christus. But again, he sensed the power in the words these strangers spoke over them.

As the couple concluded, he turned to see the little weasel-man waving them across the road onto a trail into the woods. He spoke to Salomeh first in Latin, then to Volkard in German. "I lead you to Sanctuary. I can only take you part way, but the path is clear beyond this first part. You will find safety there."

They walked in silence over logs, around boulders, and across stones. They ate from the meal provided in the sacks as the hours passed. Salomeh ate little as she huffed for breath in the effort it took her to keep pace with the men.

As the forest darkened with the setting sun, the little man stopped. He pointed to a footpath a pace ahead. "If you hurry, there should be enough light to reach Sanctuary." He turned and left them calling over his shoulder, "Watch yourself Germani—the Romans hunt you." A note of pleasure tainted his words, and the hairs on Volkard's neck again stood at attention.

Salomeh looked at him, but they were, once more reduced to hand gestures and shrugs. He moved toward the path, and she slipped her hand in his. Her touch warmed him, made him strong, and filled him with a hope that his life would now be different.

CHAPTER

NINETEEN

The day's sunlight lazed almost spent on the horizon before a whistle blared through the trees. A man in rough trousers and a sloppy shirt sprang out in front of them. Volkard tried to push Salomeh behind him to protect her from the threat, but she struggled with him talking in rapid Latin to the man. The man blocking their path kept his hand on the sheathed weapon at his hip as he looked from one of them to the other.

A shout filtered to them from farther up the trail. The man before them yelled something back, and Salomeh released a sigh. She stroked Volkard's arm and smiled at him.

A few minutes later, footsteps approached from the direction of the shouts. Another man appeared dressed much like the first. This one was older, his hair more grey than brown. He looked them both up and down. Placing a hand on the first man's shoulder, he spoke. The younger man pointed first at Salomeh, saying something that made the older man nod and then to Volkard and said something that made him scowl.

A flurry of Latin streamed from Salomeh as she clenched down on Volkard's hand. The name Christus flew over her lips a few times with Volkard's name.

Volkard shifted his weight between his feet and tried his best to be still under these men's hard stares.

The older man asked several questions, and Salomeh's answers seemed emphatic. Still holding his hand, her other arm waved out in several different directions as she did her best to convince them —of what he could only guess was her assertion he would do them no harm.

Salomeh startled at the next question, clenching his hand until his fingers tingled. She shook her head before she gave a single word reply. The query to follow made her gasp and take her hand from his, only to slam it against Volkard's chest. The words she spoke were laced with anger, and she thumped him once to make her point.

What could she possibly be telling them? Does she defend me? Make excuses for me?

The older man put his hands up in surrender, and his features softened. He inclined his head and waved them to follow.

As they walked, Salomeh pointed to the older man, "Sammanus," she said. Pointing to the other man, now following them, she said. "Treviri."

Over the next ridge, a cluster of buildings came into view. Sammanus called out, and a group of people gathered around them. Young and old, men and women, all dressed in simple garments of natural colors. Some seemed to be in families while others stood alone.

Sammanus spoke with his people and waved out his hand toward the newcomers. Their names were mentioned in the same breath as Christus. Those gathered turned to them and came forward. The women embraced Salomeh, kissing her on the cheeks, while the men offered their hands in friendship. The group quickly returned to their activities once the greetings were complete.

"Willkommen."

Volkard turned at the welcome spoken in German. A lean man with red hair, only standing as tall as Volkard's shoulder, smiled at him. He waved for Volkard to follow. As he walked toward the smaller dwellings to the left of the large central structure, Salomeh moved off to a building to the right.

The redhead touched his own chest, "Maxium."

"Volkard."

Maxium's smile grew. He pushed open a door revealing a sleeping chamber with two mats on raised platforms. He pointed to the one on the right and then himself, "Maxium." Next, he pointed to the one on the left. "Volkard."

Volkard nodded. It was nowhere near the size of the home he had made for himself in Kordt's village, but he would not be sleeping on the floor as he had done since bringing Salomeh back. A young boy of about ten ran up and handed Volkard a bundle before running off to the large central building. Maxium waved Volkard inside and shut the door but remained outside.

Dropping the items on his bed, Volkard separated them and found a pair of trousers, shirt, and boots. He put them on. Thought not a great fit—being too tight and short—they were far more desirable than the slave tunic and hated sandals. He exited the hut. Maxium considered him for a moment with a frown, and apologized, "Traurig."

Volkard shrugged. The man had said "sad" though Volkard

thought he probably meant he was sorry for the poor fit. And it seemed that was all of the German tongue the man knew, just a greeting and an smattering of single words.

Maxium waved for Volkard to follow. They came to a well where Maxium brought up a bucket of water. He washed his hands and face and stepped aside so Volkard could do the same. From there they entered the larger building.

Two long trestle tables sat surrounded by all the people living in Sanctuary. Men and women were seated side-by-side eating from common trays of meats and vegetables.

"Volkard."

He turned to see Salomeh beckon him to the farthest table. She wore a simple dress that was clearly too large for her, and her hair now hung in a single long braid. She slid along the bench making room for him to step over and sit. She placed a trencher in front of him. Memories of the last communal meal he shared flooded his mind. His parents had still been alive then.

Salomeh offered him a tray of meat—her smile radiant. As he ate in silence, the musical lilt of their spoken Latin danced around him. Salomeh talked and laughed with her new friends. Seeing her at home filled his heart. She belonged here. She turned and laid her hand over his. Her tender gaze, the curve of her lips, her warm touch, welcomed him to join her.

If only he could.

CHAPTER

TWENTY

Maxium woke Volkard the next morning, and they went to the communal meal. The cool air tingled on his bare face. He'd shaved his beard to better fit among this new clan. But it was not him.

Smiles greeted him. Hands were extended in friendship. Salomeh saved him a spot. She tipped her head and looked at him curiously causing him to brush his hand over his naked jaw.

He was welcome here among these people he couldn't speak with—his enemies—yet they treated him as a long-lost friend. It was far better than he had received anywhere since he was driven from his home.

Once the meal concluded, Maxium called his name and as they headed outside, he handed Volkard an axe. Maxium and three other men led him toward the forest, axes on their shoulders. Volkard caught Salomeh's laughter and turned to see her with an equal number of women, baskets swinging from their arms. While the men chopped, the women gathered. Their baskets overflowed with wild vegetables, berries, and nuts, while the men strained under the burden of many logs.

Later, Salomeh walked beside him pointing to various things they passed. She would name them in Latin and wait for him to name them in German. Thus, their vocabulary grew. Over the days, he laughed at her atrocious attempts to string her growing vocabulary into sentences. It made her pout, and Volkard had drawn her close to comfort her and apologize. He craved the feel of her body pressed so close to him.

Each day they would eat together and were assigned a chore in the morning hours. They passed the time of working by naming objects in one another's language. After a small midday meal, they worked around the camp repairing buildings and clothes, chopping wood into fire logs, preparing meals. Following the evening meal together, Sammanus, the graying leader, instructed them. The name of Christus was used repeatedly and Volkard marveled at how even the young sat with focused attention. Questions were asked, Sammanus answered. Heads nodded, murmurs of agreement and understanding bubbled around the room. And Volkard grew restless.

Handshakes and friendly pats on the back, smiles and joyous calls of his name always greeted him. Here, Volkard was a friend, welcomed, accepted, even though he couldn't communicate with anyone, and he didn't follow their God. It sat odd under his skin to be welcomed among strangers since he'd barely been tolerated by Kordt's clan. But it afforded him no peace. These people didn't know the manner of man he was. They didn't see the blood that stained his hands—innocent blood. Maybe even blood of their kin. They didn't know the power it held over him even now.

He went to hunt with the men, and Volkard would gut the game brought down by the men's arrows. The warm blood over his hands soothed his restless spirit. He left it on his hands and arms, only washing it off before they entered camp. Another reminder, he didn't belong here with civilized people.

Then there was Salomeh. Upturned luscious lips, gentle swing of her hips as she walked. Her tender caress of his arm as she pointed to something for him to name. No, he did not belong among these people. Not near her.

Volkard walked toward the trail leading him out of Sanctuary. Two months he had lived here. And during that time, two things became clear to him. He could never be one of them. They were people of peace, kindness, and gentleness. He was and always would be a killer; the thirst for blood yet burned in his veins. The second, and more unbearable fact haunted him—he loved Salomeh.

She spent a good portion of everyday with him. Following him out to cut wood, greeting him, and helping him dress the game he caught for the common meal. Her smile never failed to shine on him. She would take his hand at any given opportunity. And the desire she stirred in him, frightened him. She went out of her way to find him—to be with him, no matter how he tried to distance himself.

He could not have her. She was a holy one. She carried Christus in her. The God who died, now lived within her. Volkard's life with her in Sanctuary grew intolerable. For weeks, he knew he needed to leave. Finally, he could stand it no longer. This was the morning—away from good people—away from the woman who held his heart in a chokehold. Away from everything and everyone.

He slipped out before first light, but not early enough.

Pattered footfalls sounded behind him. "Volkard?"

He kept walking.

"Volkard?" she called louder.

He shut his ears to her pleas, but then she appeared in his path. Panting for breath, she put her hands on his chest to stop him.

Over these months she gained some muscle, and mended the garment they'd provided her. The now form fit of her dress pulled at his desire. He closed his eyes. *I have to get away. Find my only remaining belongings, my sword. Go far away from her.*

Her horrible German came breathless to his ears. "Volkard, walk? Wood broken? Not axe."

He shook his head.

"Volkard?"

He opened his eyes to be caught in her gaze. Her eyes, deep brown of a dark beer, held him in their watery pools. He seized hold of her with both hands on the sides of her head.

She did not startle or pull from him.

I have waited long enough. I will have her. He lowered his mouth toward hers.

Still she did not struggle against him.

His whole body cried out for her. He tightened his grip and drew her nearer.

She came.

His breaths came in rasped gasps. *To taste her—know her. This is what I wanted above all things.*

His lips close enough he could feel her breath against them, and yet she remained.

Visions of her lying bare before him as in the villa made him pant.

Snap!

Crack!

Snap!

Volkard dragged his gaze from hers. His heated breath caught in his chest.

Snap!

Crack—crack!

A cry went up, but was cut short.

Trouble!

He released Salomeh, "Run!" he ordered her with one of the Latin words she had taught him.

She turned to look toward the approaching noise.

He grabbed her by the arm and shoved her toward the safety of the structures. "Run!"

Her steps were slow at first, but as Roman soldiers came into view between the trees, she screamed and raced up the hill.

Volkard moved to stop their advance. He only saw three. If he could get a sword from one of them, he could save her—again.

The soldiers, in their white tunics and red armor, laughed at him. Two drew their swords and the third tried to go around him.

Volkard lunged for that one. He grappled with him, both trying to get control of the sword. They rolled over the leaf litter and knocked down one of the other men. Volkard came up on top of the soldier, raised his fist, and—

Pain throbbed through Volkard's head. Screams assaulted his ears.

Blackness.

CHAPTER

TWENTY-ONE

Screams. Angry shouts. Bolts of pain.

Volkard pried his eyes open. He lay on his side facing down the hill. He tried to sit up, but his arms were bound behind him. He pulled against the chains and shackles. His hands were secured too tightly together. He couldn't maneuver his hands in front of him and he couldn't break the chains.

An angry shout called out beside him.

Working his legs under him, Volkard pushed to sit on his knees. The pain radiating from the back of his head pulled bile up from his belly. Bursts of light danced before his eyes obscuring his view of the Sanctuary compound. Once he could see again, he wished he hadn't.

Bodies of the youngest and oldest lay scattered near the sleeping huts. Six soldiers stood around the central building. A shout again called out from beside him. One member of Sanctuary sat on his knees near Volkard—arms bound and face bloody. Beyond him lay other men, bound and unconscious. The man next to him, he couldn't remember his name, shouted again at the soldiers.

Volkard's gaze shifted back to the red armored men again.

Neither Salomeh nor the man's woman were anywhere to be seen.

A soldier bellowed an order toward the meeting hall.

Silence answered.

The soldier who shouted, nodded to another soldier next to him. The second man went to the fire pit and thrust in a stick with a bit of cloth wrapped on the end. Once lit, he walked to the other four soldiers and ignited their torches. All five moved toward the large common building.

Volkard roared and tried to gain his feet.

The flames took hold and grew up the walls. Screams of the women and children, not left dead outside, came from within.

On his feet, Volkard staggered forward. "Salomeh! Sal—o—meh!" His head rebelled at each shouted syllable like a wild animal against a cage.

The soldier giving orders turned and drove his fist into Volkard's middle.

Doubled over, he dropped to his knees and wretched. The soldier kicked him onto his side.

Gasping for air, Volkard rolled away from solider and got to his feet once more.

The screams from inside the meeting hall turned to shrieks. They mingled together in unintelligible terror. He couldn't distinguish one voice from another.

"Salomeh!" Volkard lunged forward slamming into the back of one of the soldiers who had helped light the blaze. The enemy lurched forward into the flames. His clothes caught fire, and he screamed as he ran from it but couldn't escape.

The heat drove Volkard back, licking at his face and singeing his regrown beard. He staggered a few steps away, bellowing against the inferno in front of him. The roof of the large structure caved in. The howl of the flames drowned out the crying. He dropped to his knees—his soul consumed in waves of misery. As the last of the building fell in on itself, so did Volkard. His forehead pressed against the heated dirt. "Salomeh, forgive me." Rage tore through him—surging up from his toes. He sat back on his heels, threw back his head, and roared from the cavern in his soul.

He pushed to his feet and charged at the nearest soldier. *If she no longer draws breath then neither will I.* With a bellow, he connected with the soldier, driving his shoulder into the man's stomach. The hilt of a Roman sword pummeled Volkard between his shoulder blades as he drove the soldier back down the hill away from the carcass of the meeting hall.

Seized by the arms, he was pulled off and thrown down on his back. Fists flew and feet fell. Latin orders were barked.

The pop and crackle of the flames calmed. The ghostly silence descended where life and laughter had been only an hour before. Death fell on his spirit as well.

He didn't care.

Let death come.

CHAPTER

TWENTY-TWO

His arms yanked in front of him and shackled, Volkard was tethered to the rest of the men from the Sanctuary, and they were led down the hill. Volkard dragged his feet through the leaf litter. None of the six captives talked. No words could be found to express their loss. No expression could do anything to bring back their women and families.

Consumed by pain as deep as losing his mother, Volkard didn't want to think, or to breathe. Why wouldn't Thor—or even her Christus—allow him to die and face the justice and eternal torment he so rightly deserved? Why take a holy one and her righteousness and allow him and his vileness to live? This world did not need another foul murderer.

He looked to the soldiers. Two led, pulling the thick chain tethering the prisoners together, two walked at their sides, and finally, one brought up the rear. Which could he provoke into killing him? Which of these soldiers would be glad to end his misery?

They rounded a corner, and the road beyond came into view. They filed onto the well-worn highway leading to the city he had visited with… her. He couldn't bring himself to even think her name. A hooded man approached from the shadows.

Volkard raised his head. The weigh station he had visited with her—where they finally talked—sat at the end of the lane—almost out of sight behind them.

The hooded man approached the soldier who had ordered the meeting hall burned. The hood dropped back revealing the weasel-faced man who had translated for them. He put out his hand, and the soldier dropped a purse of coins in it. The weasel nodded to the soldier, shook the pouch, and smiled. He smirked at Volkard as he strolled past.

Despair vanished replaced with the blood lust. If it was the last act Volkard did—he would kill the traitor who had cost her and so many others their lives. In an instant, Volkard planted his feet, wrapped his hands around the tether, and jerked with all his might.

The soldier whipped around and stumbled losing his grip on the chain.

Volkard lunged at the traitorous weasel, looped the chain of his shackles over the wretch's neck, jerked the man off his feet, and snapped his head back.

Shouts and orders blared from behind him.

The one giving orders looked down at the dead man crumpled at Volkard's feet, scooped up the purse from his lifeless hand, and put it back in his own pouch. Two of the other soldiers dragged the body into the tree line. The tether snapped taut, and they headed south.

Volkard put one foot in front of the other. He killed a man again. It gave him great pleasure, but it didn't bring back the one whose name he would never again speak or think. It didn't put breath back in her lungs or flesh on her bones. *If I can't die and know nothing as she now does… I will kill every Roman I can lay my hands on. This is my vow. Death to all of Rome.*

They walked on until the sun set and pulled off the road where the soldiers made a fire and prepared a meal. The captives received water but nothing more. The guards took shifts two at a time watching the prisoners as the others slept.

Volkard refused to sleep. Closing his eyes led only to seeing her followed by the shrieks and the flames. His heart shuddered. His lungs burned. And he prayed for death. Though he did not pray to Thor nor Christus. Both had failed him. Both had allowed her to die. He didn't know whose favor he sought now. Perhaps there were no gods at all.

Come morning, they were on their way again. Near midday they came to a Roman city. Maneuvering through the crowded streets they entered a fortification swarming with soldiers. The captives were brought in, inspected, given a simple meal, and were chained to iron rings in the wall.

The next morning a new group of soldiers came toward Volkard. As soon as they unhooked him from the wall, he flung his shackled arms over the nearest Roman neck and tried to break it as he had the weasel's. New fists assaulted his battered body and more rough hands jerked Volkard off the man. Too soon he again stood tethered behind soldiers. None of the men who survived from Sanctuary were with him now. The prisoners marched out in two long rows of ten deep. Volkard walked near the front behind two other men. A lanky brown-haired man stood chained to his left. They headed south through the town and out into the paved Roman road.

Once outside the city walls, the man beside him said something. Within a few moments another word in a different language filtered to him. Finally, Volkard heard, "Need prayer?" in German.

Volkard spit on the ground, "I curse all gods!"

"Oh, then above all you need the prayer of reconciliation with Christus."

Volkard jerked out of line and threw himself at the man beside him. "Christus? Christus did all this. He allowed one of His own to be burned alive. I hate Him. I will always hate Him or what He allowed to happen to her!"

The soldiers jerked the two men apart as the line started forward once again.

"Christus took one of His own—out of the world where His followers are burned alive—and has taken her to His bosom where she will never again know pain or tears. Where she will live in the unmatched joy of His presence for all of eternity. This is a God you will hate until your last breath?"

"Do not speak to me of your God." He spit on the ground again.

"I will not speak to you. I will pray for you. What is your name friend?"

Volkard would not respond.

"Lord God, my Savior, this new friend of mine is hurting."

"Shut up!"

"One of Your children, who was dear to him, has been lost to this life. She now resides with You, her Savior and her God, but her loss is a burden to this child of Yours. Show him Your love, Father. Show him You have a plan and purpose. One that is only for his good—for a future full of hope. We ask this in the name of Christus."

Volkard grunted his disdain—but he couldn't deny the power in the words said over him. A power he had felt before. A power he now despised.

CHAPTER

TWENTY-THREE

"My name is Marcellus. What is your name, friend?" The miles passed, and the man chained next to him wouldn't stop talking.

Volkard did not answer. But the chatter would not relent. At last he said. "Do not speak to me. I want nothing of you or your God. I want only to kill every Roman I meet."

"You know, my friend, Christus has done mighty things for you. You may not wish to know Him, but He desires greatly to know you."

"Then He should not have killed her!"

Marcellus sighed. "God did not kill her, my friend. Evil killed her."

"If He is as powerful a God as you say, He should have saved her."

"Oh, but He did. She is forever safe."

Volkard growled.

"Let me tell you of Christus. Then you can decide for yourself."

As words tumbled from his mouth in a long continuous stream, Volkard glanced at the other prisoners. None spoke. Any who tried to put voice to their thoughts were struck until they fell silent. Marcellus continued unhampered. The others trudged along, heads down, feet dragging and occasionally stumbling forward after a tug on the tether. Marcellus strolled along unconcerned by the shackles or the soldiers.

"Why don't they shut you up?" Volkard asked.

"When I was captured and knew I would be transported to Arretium, I asked God to put a man who walked next to me who He wanted me to talk to. You, my friend, are that man. God Himself chose you of all these men to hear His Good News. And He prepared me in advance to speak your tongue, my Germani friend."

Volkard grumbled his words, "But *why* do the soldiers allow you to speak since no others are allowed—in truth they are punished if they utter a word."

A chuckle of laughter bubbled from the thin man. "I have heard the guards talking. They know you do not wish me to speak, so they see it as part of your torment, my friend."

Volkard tested the slack of his tether to see if he could reach Marcellus to silence him himself.

The story of Christus continued. Volkard couldn't reconcile a God who left paradise to become a mortal babe, only to grow to a man and be put to a Roman traitor's death. But to add to such unbelievable events, Marcellus asserted this Christus—this God-man—had risen from the dead and walked on earth among His followers before returning to the heavenlies. Such was impossible. Volkard wanted to stop up his ears against the wild tale the man spun without relenting or tiring.

Mile by mile, the man would not rest. The only time he didn't speak about his God or the God-man's teachings, either his mouth was full, or he slept. Marcellus remained an unstoppable force. He saw it as his mission to convert Volkard to be a follower of what Marcellus called the Way—a follower of Christus.

As they sat against a tree eating their daily rations, Volkard interrupted his stream of endless words. "I will not become a follower of your God. I reject even the gods of my youth. None have served to aid me. I have known nothing but death and killing —loss greater than you can imagine."

Marcellus rested his head back against the same tree, and he stared out at nothing. "My father was captured and sent to the coliseum. I watched as wild beasts tore him apart. He praised his Savior with his last breath. I fled with my wife and children to the north. On our journey, my beautiful Lidia fell into the hands of evil men, and they abused her. She never recovered from the injuries they inflicted upon her and died days later in my arms."

He wiped a tear from his cheek—the chains of his shackles clanking with the movement. "My precious baby girl died within the month, and my son half a year later leaving me alone to draw breath on this cruel earth. I stayed with my brother on the Limes, and his house fell to Germani warriors. Some were carried off as they needed laborers." He turned to look at Volkard, a slim smile pulling at the corners of his lips. "This is where I learned to speak as one of you."

"With so much loss, how can you continue to believe in the mercy of your God?"

"I know my family is cradled in my Lord's arms in heaven. My God has sustained me in all things. I yet draw breath to speak as

His witness, and I still know peace and joy. Serving God is my greatest delight and honor. The benefits I receive far outweigh my trial in this temporary life. This life lasts but a moment, but the rewards will go on for all eternity."

The passion of his words stirred Volkard's aching soul. But days of walking and listening to him had worn a raw spot on his sore nerves. "I have listened to you for seventeen days, I will not be bent to your faith. What must I do to silence you?"

"I will make you a deal, my friend. Let me prove to you God seeks after you like a fearsome hound. I feel it in my very bones— God is calling to you."

"How can you prove the will of God?"

"When we reach Arretium, we will be taken to the slave market to be sold."

"I thought Arretium a military station?"

"It is, but it is also part of a sprawling city now. This is how you will know God's desire for you. If, when we are sold, we go to the same master, you will know God wishes for you to hear more of Him until you surrender to His will for your life."

Volkard looked over the man from the top of his shaggy head down his narrow form with is rope thick arms and legs. "Not likely we would be chosen by the same master."

"True. You are built for hard labor, the quarries, the belly of a ship, or—most likely—a gladiator." He nodded his head. "Yes, you will be a gladiator. And when I am bought to be trained as a gladiator too—by the lanista of the same ludus—then you will know God pursues you, my friend."

Volkard rolled on his side and curled to sleep. "It will never happen, but if it will buy your silence, I accept."

"There is another part of your agreement you are neglecting."

"What would that be?"

"I will hear your name, and then you will hear no more from me until we enter the ludus—the gladiator school—together as fellow novice," Marcellus said with a yawn.

"Volkard."

CHAPTER

TWENTY-FOUR

True to his word, Marcellus made not a single sound. The blessed silence was only interrupted by the steady march of the soldiers' feet and the scuffed dragging steps of the prisons. In this void, Volkard reached for his blood lust—the one thing he had hoped to outrun—the part of himself he hated. Now he clung to it like a child to a cherished plaything. He tried to envision his guards lying bloody at his feet, but the images were fleeting and did not ignite or feed his hunger. He thought through his attack, but it was repeatedly interrupted by Marcellus' words about Christus."

He tossed his head and focused on which guard would be the easiest to over power, but his thoughts were captured by the image of this God bleeding on a Roman cross. The bloodied figure looked down on Volkard and whispered words fell on him.

"I know your name, and this I do for you, Volkard of the Heruli."

Volkard stumbled. He was only saved from falling by the quick action of Marcellus. Volkard glanced at the man once the steady rhythm of his steps had returned. Marcellus' head was bowed. His eyes hooded—only open enough to see if his next step was safe.

His lips moved without end, though no words escaped to foul the air.

What did Marcellus do? Rehearse the words he would use to convince Volkard? The more he studied the religious man, the more Volkard feared Marcellus prayed over him. *I want nothing of your God. Do not pray for my soul—I seek no redemption. I want only blood.*

Turning his attention back to his goal, Volkard looked to the gladius hanging at each soldier's hip and the shorter daggers tucked in their belts. The damage he could do—

A woman, with black hair braided down her back, walked by the marching prisoners. A basket carried on her hip, she looked up and smiled a sad smile at them as they passed.

Volkard saw *her* again—the one he would not mention. It would have broken her heart to know he wanted to avenge her death on all he met. *Good it is for me—she no longer draws breath.* Saying such—even to himself—cut through him, adding to his pain and constricting his lungs until they burned for the air denied to them.

They entered the noisy crowded city of Arretium a few days later. Volkard couldn't see the appeal of life with so many bodies bumping into each other, or being locked within such massive stones.

The prisoners waited an hour in a wood pen before they were led to a raised platform one at a time. Several men came and inspected each one in turn and the captives were made to stand naked before those gathered. A placard hung around each man's neck which Marcellus said the important information about each of them such as nationality, and abilities. Because Volkard was considered an imported salve, one of his feet was whitened with chalk.

The slave trader, known as a Venalitti, called out things that Volkard could not understand as others stepped up to inspect him. A few thumped his chest. Others forced him to open his mouth. When Volkard tried to bite at an offensive finger examining his teeth, the sting of a whip across his back came before a collar with a stick attached to it was fastened around his neck. A man nearly his size held him firm for further inspection.

His skin boiled, beaten by the sun and heated from within by his fury. Volkard envisioned killing each man who passed before him. He would kill them all in a different manner—strangled, run through, arms pulled off, head ripped from his shoulders.

Once sold, both men and women were given tunics and returned to a pen until their new masters collected them.

At the end of the day Volkard walked, still shackled, surrounded by gladiators—Marcellus at his side. The man's chin rose—still not higher than Volkard's shoulder—a satisfied smirk on his lips. "We are to be gladiators."

"How did you manage to get them to purchase you to serve the glory of Rome as a gladiator?" Volkard said with disgust.

"I did nothing. It is as I told you, brother. God seeks after your soul."

"I am not your brother."

"Well, not yet." Marcellus' smile was so large Volkard pulled against his chains in an attempt to slap it from his smug face.

The iron-gate clicked as the lock turned. They walked into an arena and stood before the lanista, the manager of the ludus. Volkard and Marcellus were among a group of about ten men. Before the toga wrapped man on the balcony above started speaking, Marcellus cleared his throat and said something to the powerful man.

The man looked down, his gaze shifting from Marcellus to Volkard and back again. He nodded and began speaking. After a few words, Marcellus began whispering to Volkard.

"The owner, Lanista Arturos, says, 'You are my property—whether prisoner or freemen who have sold themselves for a term of service to prove themselves. You will live in locked cells until you become trusted trained gladiators. You will receive three meals, and you will train all day every day. Those who are found unworthy will be sent to the arena to die in a show for the great citizens of Roma. Those who take to their training will fight for the glory of Roma.'"

Lanista Arturos disappeared into the structure behind him.

Marcellus said, "The doctores—those who will serve as our trainers," he pointed to the tunic clade men standing crossed armed in front of their ranks.

The man in the middle barked an order.

"We are to proceed to the baths," Marcellus fell in line with Volkard at his back. They walked to the back of the arena and enter titled rooms. They were stripped but left in their shackles.

A growl rumbled in Volkard's throat at the humiliation.

"The baths are a luxury of Rome. It shows their power over water. Enjoy the cold water of the frigidarium. We go next to the tepidarium, and finally, end in the hot caldarium where a slave will scrape the dirt and oils from the skin with a strigle." The men moved through the rooms ending in one suffocating with heat— steam hanging heavy enough in the air to make breathing difficult.

"I will not allow a man to touch my uncovered body."

"Lord God, calm Volkard's spirit. Let him not act rashly in this simple act of cleaning."

"Stop praying foolish words over me."

"But we are instructed to pray without ceasing. In all things bring your needs before the Lord who cares for you. And did we not have an agreement? If we ended in the same location, I could speak to you about my God, who will someday soon, be your God."

Marcellus said something to the slave approaching with a smooth stick in one hand and a rag in the other.

The young man nodded and motioned for Volkard to put out his arms straight in front of him. "Be a man of reason, Volkard. How can you enact the vengeance you seek on all Romans if you kill this one lowly slave who has no more choice than you do at this moment?"

Volkard stamped down his fury, tucking it away in a dark corner of his soul where he could nurture it and allow it to fester. He would save it for a better time when he could kill more of his enemy.

The action of the stick scrapping over his skin reminded Volkard of *her*. She had tried to clean herself this way in his home. Even this simple thing brought him pain.

The three levels of bathing complete, the men moved to another room with stone tables. "How often must we endure such treatment?" Volkard asked as he was directed to lie on his stomach on one of the tables.

"Once a day at least." Marcellus took the table beside him.

Oil drizzled over his back and another man began working it into his skin as he kneaded every muscle. Again, Volkard growled. His stomach clenched because of the man touching him. And the Romans called *him* the barbarian.

"Peace, friend."

A new man entered the room, and he came to inspect each man. Volkard looked to Marcellus.

"He is a healer. He determines our health and ability to fight."

"And what will you do when he rejects you? You are half the size of any other man I have seen in this place."

Marcellus smiled. "And what will you do when he says I am fit as any of you?"

After the inspection, they were given a strip of cloth. "And what am I supposed to do with this?"

Marcellus tied two corners together around his waist. "It is a cloth to cover your loins, friend." He pulled the long dangling end up between his legs, worked it under the knot he had tied, draped it over the top, and secured it with a wide leather belt. "This is what we will fight in," Marcellus told him. As he took a tunic from a slave, a trainer unlocked his shackles long enough for him to slide it over his head, and he was secured once more. "At all times we are not fighting or training, we will wear the tunic.

Every moment, Volkard hated something new about the Romans and the life he would now be living. They moved next to a larger room lined with long trestle tables. They reminded him of those that were now only ashes in the woods to the north. The prisoners were given instructions at the door.

Marcellus turned and whispered over his shoulder before stepping inside. "We are to eat in silence—everything we are given."

Volkard plopped down on a bench and glared at the plate placed in front of him. The room filled with men. Not one sound, other than wooden spoons scrapping on plate, could be heard. Here, at least, Marcellus could not preach to him.

Volkard picked at the food before him. Some looked familiar —a gruel and barley breads. Other items looked to be inedible. One of the trainers stood before him, arms crossed, and scowled. Volkard shoved the food in his mouth and swallowed. Some of the food could be tolerated, others turned his stomach. He washed the odd flavors from his mouth with water. Beer, wine, and ale was not allowed.

The meal concluded. They moved to the second floor where they were locked into a cell with two cots on opposite walls.

Marcellus moved to the far wall, stretched out on the bed. "Lord, we thank You for this day. For Your providence in bringing us here together so I may continue to speak to Volkard of Your Way."

Volkard threw himself onto his bed. "You thank your God for sending us to a place where we will be trained to be better killers. This is what your God wants?"

"I will kill no man." The words were low, calm, and steeled in determination. "Now sleep. We rise early to begin our training." Marcellus turned on his side and dropped off to sleep in near the next breath.

"I will not follow Christus! I will not bend to His will. I have vowed vengeance on all Romans." He stared up at the dark ceiling listening to the thump of his aching heart. He had planned to leave her. One day earlier and he would have never known her fate. And this life would not be his. But he couldn't leave then, and he couldn't stop mourning her now.

He looked to the high window of his cell. Moonlight reflected off a wispy cloud. "If Marcellus speaks truth," he whispered, "and she now resides in Your realm, please tell her I am sorry. I should have done more to protect her."

As sleep crept in around him, he saw her shining face like the day he found her kneeling in prayer in the villa. Her smile spread wide. 'Christus loves you, Volkard.' He released his spirit into the abyss of night hearing those words echo within him.

CHAPTER

TWENTY-FIVE

Volkard raised his rudus. It was a ridiculous substitute for the sword he would have in the arena. Nothing more than a short round stick with a handle that didn't have the weight or the reach of his German sword or even the Roman gladius he would eventually use for the Romans' entertainment. How was this inadequate tool supposed to prepare him?

"Germanicus, you have opened yourself up to attack in your middle," his trainer Ennius barked.

In the months he had been in the ludus, Volkard had been given a new name, Marcellus shoved Latin in him like the trainers plied him with food, and he grew in his skill at how to kill a man in spite of the rudus.

Volkard grunted and slashed out with his weapon, proving he was not open to attack. He knocked the rudus from his opponent's hand and forced him to the ground.

"You will not always be able to rely on your brute strength, Germanicus." Ennius warned as he called over another. "Faust, show Germanicus the art of small and precise movements."

The two men sparred as the wooden weapons banged together. The hollow echoes of their mock blades filled their corner of the arena. They matched one another blow for blow, slash for slash, thrust for thrust. Faust faked to the right and tried to kick Volkard's leg out from under him. Volkard was no fool. He dropped to his other knee, and while Faust leaned in for the attempted deathblow, Volkard burst to his feet catching his opponent in the stomach with his shoulder. Volkard picked the other man off his feet and drove him down on his back. One hand on the man's throat, he raised his rudus to deliver the final blow.

Hands seized Volkard's arms and pulled him off his fallen opponent. "Enough!"

Volkard stepped back, brushing the sand from his sweat covered flesh.

"Germanicus, you are still a barbarian. You will never truly learn the finer points of good fighting," Faust said.

"I have enough skill to take down a pretender like you," Volkard said.

Faust took a swing at Volkard who dodged it and threw one of his own. Volkard connected snapping the man around. He continued driving his fist into Faust's lower back.

Again, Volkard was yanked from the other man. One of his captors whispered in his ear, "He is a freeman."

"He sold himself into this life. He trains with the rest of us." Volkard fought to free himself of the hold.

"No, Germanicus." The man restraining him shook his head. "You will never be on the same footing as him. A few fights won, and he will be free to walk from here. It is not likely you will ever see freedom again."

The two trainers held Volkard so he could neither fight back nor protect himself. Faust delivered a blow to his ribs driving air from his lungs. Two more quick strikes to his middle kept the breath from returning. Faust next drove his fist deeper into Volkard's gut, doubling him over and nearly bringing up his lunch. Faust knew better than to break any bones. Volkard was another man's property and Faust would pay if Volkard was too injured to fight. Wheezing for air and straining against the hands detaining him, Volkard didn't have time to think as the strike came up under his chin slamming his head back. Faust ended his retaliation with a final blow to Volkard's face. Blood flowed down over his lips as Faust moved off to another training area. Volkard dropped to one knee gasping for breath.

Marcellus helped him to the physicians where his injuries were assessed and treated. "You know the freemen are of more value. They will leave to enjoy their fame in but a couple of years. Why continue to provoke them?"

"He goaded me. Besides, a broken nose and more bruises are of little consequence. The others are all threatened by my skill and my size—even the trainers. I have the skill to kill them all. Put a gladius in my hand—"

Marcellus clouted him in the jaw. The gentle punch still made Volkard's jaw ache. Marcellus looked all around for witnesses. He switched back to German, something he did whenever they were alone in order to instruct Volkard of ways of Christus. "You know these walls have ears. Do you wish to be thrown in the arena now with no hope of surviving?" He thumped his fist into Volkard's shoulder to drive home his point. Though Volkard trained to be a hoplomachi gladiator, one of the larger heavily-armored fighters.

Marcellus trained to be an eques, a lithe gladiator who fought from horseback. Still, there was power in his punch. "You are meant for more than this death ring. One day you will walk from these walls a free man… and there will be no blood on your hands."

Volkard stood from the treatment table and walked toward the baths. His day was done, and he would soak in the hot water—something he had grown to tolerate with some small measure of pleasure. Master Arturos knew the value of his fighters only remained high if he ensured they stayed physically fit. Whenever a fighter received injuries severe enough to warrant a trip to the physicians, they were to rest for the remainder of the day.

As the two men parted, Volkard to the bath and Marcellus back to his training, Volkard asked. "Have you become an oracle, Marcellus?"

"God has promised me it is true, Volkard. You have but to trust in Him."

"There is always that demand of your God."

Volkard opened the door of his new cell. Now a novicius for half a year, he was like most—resigned to his fate as gladiator until he died. Shackles were no longer required and his cell was left unlocked. It would be the most freedom Volkard believed he would ever receive. Other than the lock and not sharing the space, little differed in his new chamber from his first one. A single bed, a chair, and a small table sat within. Volkard glanced over his shoulder to Marcellus who walked into his chamber, which sat opposite his across the hall.

"God is good, my friend."

Volkard leaned against his doorframe and crossed his arms. "Marcellus, if your God is so great, why has he not granted us our freedom."

"There is a purpose for us here, Volkard. Something you or I still must accomplish."

Volkard grunted and stomped inside. He plopped in his chair and looked out the square window high on the wall. A cloud floated by and his mind drifted with it. *She* would have liked Marcellus. All these months past, and he still could not bear her name even in thought. He pushed all thought of her aside while the ache in his heart pricked him again.

He looked back toward his door turning his thoughts back to Marcellus. Despite this harsh and violent place, he never failed to have a smile and a kind word for everyone. Though most of the experienced gladiators and novices thought him soft, they afforded him a level of respect reserved for only a few.

Volkard lay his head back and closed his eyes. What would *she* think of him now? Even in the mock battles that prepared them for death, Volkard didn't suffer the rage in his blood that drove him to kill. He fought and prevailed more times than not, but he had no love for it. In truth, he felt little to nothing. He rose each day, ate, trained, ate, trained, bathed, ate, and slept. The days were unending monotony. Nothing stirred him since *she* died.

A knock sounded at his door drawing him from his musing.

"Enter," Volkard lifted his head and opened his eyes expecting to see Marcellus coming to instruct him in the Way. He sprang out of the chair at the woman standing seductively in his doorway. "What do you want?"

She smiled and started to pull her short-draped garment off a shoulder. "I am for you, gladiator."

"No!" He stomped toward her and yanked her garment up.

Her lower lip pooched out in an ugly pout. "Would you prefer a boy?"

"No! By the gods, no." He reached for the door to show her out.

Her hand ran down his arm causing him to jerk from her touch. "I will provide you with great pleasure, gladiator."

"I do not need your service. You can leave—now." He started to pull the door open.

She stood between him and the entrance blocking her forced removal. "If you worry about a lover back home, they have probably replaced you by now."

Volkard seized her by the upper arm. "I have no lover—back home or anywhere else."

She whimpered, shying from him as though he would strike her.

He loosened his grip. "Woman, you may comfort many a man. I don't need you. If that changes, I will send for you." He pulled her back and opened the door. "Good-bye." He pushed her outside.

Marcellus stood outside his door directing another woman along as well. The men nodded to one another and closed their doors.

Volkard blew out his candle and laid on his cot with his hands behind his head. The prostitute's hair was long and dark like *hers* had been. This woman would have stood shorter than *her* by a few fingers, but they were both slight and endowed with a pleasing figure. This strange woman, however, did not have a pull on is flesh—not like *she* had. Again, only hollowness filled him.

He closed his eyes. Nothing stirred him except one desire. Suicide was forbidden above all other crimes in the ludus. Those who attempted it and failed were punished without mercy.

Still the thought enticed him. He would be better off dead—like *her*.

CHAPTER

TWENTY-SIX

Volkard did his best to follow his friend's advice as they trained day after day, week after week, month after month. Men who had completed their first year of training went off to fight in the arena. Some never to return. New slaves joined their ranks. The faces changed but never the routine. Each day lay filled with training to kill another.

Marcellus walked beside Volkard as they followed the other gladiators into the villa on the hill above their school. "The last night we are novices, my friend." A somber tone flavored his words causing Volkard to look at him.

Volkard kept his voice low. "We have trained for near a year. Should it not be time we prove ourselves in the arena?"

"How is it proving one's self to kill another—not in defense of family or even your own life—but for entertainment."

"Is that not why we train—to fight to defend our lives?"

"This is not defense of life. This is evil." Marcellus shook his head.

Before Volkard could question him further, they were ushered into the grand Roman dining room. Cushions lined the floor around the many low tables. Heavy drapes shrouded the windows blocking out the light of the setting sun. The tables overflowed with sweet meats exotic fruits. Women stood waiting against the walls.

As the men entered, each woman came to hang on an arm of a man of their choice. These were not prostitutes, but women of standing—though you would never know the difference by their behavior. Their gowns pooled to the floor and their heads held high. Their patron stood at the head of the room as the women pulled their men to positions around the table.

"Hello novices, and welcome to my home for your first coena libera, a party for novices the night before their fight. I am Senator Antony Flavius Ventrex, your host at this celebration. Some of you will not be alive come this time tomorrow." He lifted his cup. "So gladiators, eat, drink, enjoy of the pleasures of this night, and tomorrow if the gods will it so—die well."

The gladiators raised their cups in salute and honor of their host. They sat and ate leisurely conversing with the other guests. Volkard, for the first time, missed the silence of the barrack's dining hall. The women on either side of him fawned over him. Their breathy voices assaulted his ears, while their heated stares roamed over his entire body—along with their wandering hands.

Marcellus sat across the table from him, women draped on either side of him as well. The seductive companions tried to feed Marcellus dangling a grape and share their cups of wine. He answered each question with as few words as possible and focused all his attention on the plate of food in front of him, but he spent more time pushing around than eating.

Volkard followed Marcellus' lead and did his best to ignore the advances of the women without offending the patron or his important guests.

The meal dragged on for hours. Volkard fought exhaustion, deeper than a day in the practice arena, long before the entertainment began. Dancers came first, swinging their hips, their hands provocatively caressing their own bodies and those of the men seated nearest them. Some of the novices and their clinging women slipped away. Volkard would not be moved.

Toward the end of the evening the women pestering him wandered off and latched themselves to other eager men. There was a time of wrestling matches amongst some of the gladiators. Even the host wrestled with one. Of course, the senator won. Finally, the men were escorted back to the barracks.

Marcellus fell to the back of the pack, quiet and somber.

"Are you worried about tomorrow?" Volkard asked.

He looked up with a smile, which spoke only of peace. "No, Volkard. Tomorrow I go home."

Volkard thought on this for several steps. "Do you think to win your freedom with your first bout?"

"No brother, I go home to my Savior."

"You have trained well. You are likely to win against any opponent. There is great advantage in fighting from horseback. With its speed and your longer sword you could defeat me."

Marcellus slowed his steps creating more distance between them and the gladiators walking in front of them. The next time he spoke, he did so in German. "Volkard, hear me, and do not speak against my decision. I will not walk out of the arena tomorrow. I have taught you all that I know of Christus and all His ways. Now the choice is up to you."

"I say again you can prevail."

"I do not want to prevail against any man who is not prepared to meet his Creator." He glanced at Volkard. "I know where I go in death. My Savior awaits me and my wife and children as well."

"You are so sure of this?"

"I have no doubt. God allowed me to be captured after the loss of all I loved to teach you, my friend. I tell you again, God seeks after you. Do you not feel His call?"

Volkard did not speak as they ambled along the halls and up the stairs to their chambers. He stopped outside his door and leaned against the wall as the others entered their rooms. Many wished them both success or a good death in the coming day. All the doors now closed, the two men stood alone in the hallway, Volkard spoke.

"I admit, I have felt a power when you call on the name of Christus—unlike anything I have ever known in calling upon Thor or the old gods. There has been a peace about me when I hear your words. I believe Christus is a God of power."

Marcellus slumped against his door.

"Perhaps He is the only true God, Marcellus. Most likely He is the one God, as you say. But if I surrender to His will, my vow of vengeance against all Romans will be forfeit."

"I am Roman. Do you vow to kill me, Volkard? What of the dear woman who stole your heart? Would she view you as a man of honor for your vow?"

"No," Volkard growled.

"I go into the arena tomorrow knowing the love of God. I trust Him to carry me through to paradise. He is ever faithful. What of you, brother? There are no guarantees for you—even with your great strength and skill. There is always the possibility you will not walk out of the arena yourself. Where will your soul spend eternity?"

"In your hell I would imagine, Marcellus. There is too much blood on my hands."

"If Christus cannot forgive your sin, then I stand before Him unforgiven as well. God does not weigh sins as men do, Volkard. Anything that misses His mark of perfection—whether it be a lie, a theft, or a murder—it is all the same in the eyes of God."

Volkard pulled his hands from behind his back and looked at them. "Why do I still see them drenched in blood?"

"Because you do not see them with God's eyes. He alone can change you, Volkard—from the inside." Marcellus opened his door. "I will pray for you all night, my friend."

CHAPTER

TWENTY-SEVEN

The cheer of the crowd vibrated the beams holding up the stadium floor. Wild animals roared in their cages as the men sat in silence on benches lining the wall. Volkard rolled his shoulders to ward off the tension.

Marcellus was the calmest of them all, head tipped back against the bricks, eyes closed and breathing with ease.

Two of the others, Brutus and Gaius stood and paced the length of the room.

"Sit down," Faust barked.

"If it settles them to pace, let them be—it could be their last moments," Junius shot back.

"We've been trained. If you die, do so with honor. Death comes to all. Today it comes to some of us," Faust said.

Another man hung his head and cried.

Junius and Faust stood and challenged one another.

Volkard rose and put a hand on each man's shoulder. "Peace brothers; there is enough rage in the stadium above. Save your energy to stay alive."

Shrieks, roars, and cheers mingled together in a cacophony of decadent vile noise. The men within the chamber froze. Listening to the deaths above and the applause of those watching, made some shrink back against the walls—two others wretched on the dirt floor. And another joined the one who cried.

"Stop your weeping. You're men, not blubbering women."

Again, Volkard confronted Faust, "They are young. When the time comes, their training will come back to them, and they will fight. Let them mourn in this moment."

"Gladiators, come!" a trainer called.

They filed out walking in silence in the narrow dark passageway of the hypogeum below the arena. Prisoners cowered in the first few cells they passed. Lions, bears, and other beasts snarled through bars and roared before the men climbed the slim twisting steps to the level of the arena. They walked into a chamber with a gate leading out onto the stadium floor. Only the sound of a few stifled sniffles accompanied them.

Volkard and a select group of others received assistance into the last of their armor. Shields and weapons were distributed, and the men entered the arena, with a shout to Hercules, the patron god of gladiators, to stand before the senator who hosted the party the night before.

They raised their weapons and called out in a responding chant. "We who are about to die, salute you."

Cheers assaulted Volkard's ears until he squinted his eyes against the onslaught. All but two of the gladiators turned and walked back out of the stadium. Once they re-entered the upper chamber, most turned and watched the first bout. A favored one of the men, Faust, the citizen who had sold himself into service for fame and glory alone, prepared for one of the final battles of his term. He faced off with a slave who fought in his third match.

The crowd chanted for their favorite fighter.

"Faust. Faust. Fau-st!"

"Gaius. Gaius."

The men circled one another. With gladius and shield versus trident and net, each man tried to overpower the other. Thrust and dodge. Swing and duck. The clank of metal against metal echoed through the arena but neither found the advantage. One charged— the other feigned away and countered from behind.

As the two grappled, the others stood at the gate and watched —all except Marcellus. He sat on the bench as before, head back and eyes closed.

In the stadium, the professional gladiator subdued the less experienced man. Both were spared with a raised fist of the senator, and they returned panting and dripping in sweat to the chamber.

The next gladiators were called forth. "Felix. Junius. Marcellus."

Marcellus stood in a fluid calm motion, collected his sword, and moved toward the door.

"Can I not persuade you to fight and live?" Volkard whispered.

"I hear my Savior calling me, your words cannot outshine His sweet song." He passed Volkard and took another step. He turned back for one last message in German. "He calls for you too. He has something beyond what you can dream or imagine, and He loves you, brother."

Marcellus moved into the arena, mounted a dull brown steed, and faced off with two other heavily armored, sword wielding gladiators on foot—the type of gladiator favored by most Romans. Marcellus circled around his opponents. Gladius swinging, Felix slashed at the horse and drove Marcellus back. Junius approached on Marcellus' right and tried to take advantage of the distraction. Marcellus deflected the blow with his shield. Felix sprang in from his other side and pulled him from the saddle. Marcellus came to his feet without his shield as the horse darted away. Marcellus' gaze darted to the heavens before returning to his opponents. Junius swung his sword in an arc and—instead of moving back—Marcellus stepped into the swing.

The blow opened Marcellus' throat dropping him to his knees and he fell flat on his face.

Volkard turned and moved to the back of the chamber. Bracing his elbows on his knees, he intertwined his fingers and bowed his head in a whispered prayer. "Christus, accept another one of Your faithful ones. He lived and died praising Your name."

CHAPTER

TWETNTY-EIGHT

A hand pressed against Volkard's shoulder drawing him from the loss of his friend. He stood and moved without thought. Helmed and sword in hand, he entered the stadium as one of the last fights for the day. He was matched with another similar gladiator—the only like pairing of gladiators all day. The men were introduced, and the cheers of Volkard's arena name, Germanicus, clanged between his helmet and his ears. He faced Belen, a Greek he had trained with many times. They were equally matched in size and strength—but not experience. Though Volkard stepped in the arena for the first time, Belen was a veteran of the fights.

Belen's blade smashed against Volkard's shield. The vibration shuddered up his arm and brought Volkard to life. He lashed out and their swords clashed repeatedly, but the roar of the crowds drowned out the clang of metal. Volkard drove the man back. All his personal losses bubbled up from a deep well in his soul. From within, it surged over his head, down his arm, and onto Belen's shield—a payment for his long dead father in a war with tribes who came down from farther north.

Another blow sword to sword—payment for his mother who died of hunger after they were driven from their home.

Clank! Volkard smashed into the greave covering Belen' shin—for the rejection he suffered by dozens of southern tribes.

Clang, clang, clang! Volkard drove the man nearly to the stadium wall thinking of *her* burning to death.

Belen spun to get away from the wall, but Volkard caught his foot and Belen landed hard on his back.

Volkard raised his sword high, ready to deliver the death blow —final payment for the death of his friend Marcellus.

Belen squirmed dislodging his helmet. He stared up at death—knowing his end had come.

The roar of the crowd descended on Volkard like a mighty wave. Hand gestures of thumbs pointing to throats called for Belen's death. The longing to draw blood, fed the craving gnawing at him intensified until it stole his breath and rocked him back on his heels.

One day you will walk from these walls a free man—and there will be no blood on your hands. Marcellus' words drown out the crowd and dropped him back another step.

Belen popped to his feet, snatched up his sword, and came after Volkard with the same ferocity aimed at him a moment ago. Volkard fell back before him, but he matched him blow for blow.

Perhaps Marcellus was correct—death was better.

One day you will walk *from these walls a* free *man.*

Walk from these walls. Walk…

Volkard planted his feet, and they went strike for strike, thrust for thrust, shield to shield, and sword against shield. *Clang! Clang! Clang!.* They battled without advantage until Volkard's arm vibrated and ached.

The senator called an end to the match announcing a draw between the combatants.

Volkard's arm hung limp at his side. They acknowledged their patron's favor with a bow before they moved to the chamber with the other gladiators. Stripped of his armor, and breathing hard, Volkard pressed his bare back against the wall and let the coolness of the stones kiss his heated skin. Glancing around the chamber as the men disarmed and stacked their weapons, Volkard noted Marcellus was not the only one who had lost his life this day.

Volkard walked alone at the back of the line of gladiators as they returned to the barracks. Some talked—recounting close scrapes while others shared the joy of a win and another day of life. He didn't say a word. Standing away from the others as they related the events of the day to those who had not gone to the stadium, Volkard progressed through the three bathing chambers. He missed Marcellus. He wanted to hear a comforting word from the God who loved him.

Lounging on a massage table as the slave worked the knots out of his tight muscles, he heard Marcellus' voice. "Christus said, 'Peace I leave with you. In the world you will have trouble, but fear not I have overcome the world.' Trust in Him, Volkard, and you too can know this peace."

He knew that peace was there for the taking, but he could not feel it as he had in the past.

They moved to the dining room, but he ate little. This night no one force him, and Volkard left to return to his chamber early.

Volkard plodded up the stairs wishing to hear Marcellus' cheerful voice. He stared at his friend's door wondering what manner of man would occupy the room across the hall now. Not one with as fine a character Volkard was sure.

He turned and pushed open his own door and found a woman reclined across his bed. Remaining in the doorway, Volkard scowled at her. "Leave."

"But I am your reward, gladiator. Come and celebrate." She stroked the mattress beside her.

"My friend died. I celebrate nothing."

"But you did not die—"

"I deserved death. More than he. Go. I'm tired."

"We do not need to lie together, gladiator." Her breathy voice held no allure for him—it berated his skin like coarse sand. "I can tend to your needs in other ways."

"Get out! Must I remove you or will you leave?"

She eased up to a sitting position as her gaze slid up and down his body. She rose to her feet and sauntered to him, swinging her hips with slow calculated precision. She approached him gliding her hand down his chest. "I can't change your mind?"

He gripped her by the arm, pulled her through the door, and shoved her down the hall. Entering his chamber, he slammed the door behind him. He flopped down on his bed. It still smelled of her flowery perfume.

He jumped to his feet and paced his cell. His skin crawled as though beetles crept beneath the surface. He scratched, but it did no good. An hour of circuits and he wearied of the movement. Returning to his mat, he flipped over the thin padding and lay down again. Sleep never found him, and he rose with the sun and went to the practice arena to train.

CHAPTER

TWENTY-NINE

Sparring with a newly purchased slave, the young man flailed and hammered Volkard in the temple. The hollow echo rattled his thoughts and stirred his ire. Volkard flew at him. Sticking his foot behind the boy's staggering steps, Volkard's fists thrust into the clumsy oaf's shoulders. He knocked the boy to the ground. As he sputtered for air, Volkard raised a fist to pummel the boy into the dust.

His opponent's eyes nearly popped from his head. Beads of sweat shone on his forehead and above his lip.

One day you will walk from these walls a free man—and there will be no blood *on your hands.*

Volkard stood up straight, gaze locked with the quaking novice. No blood. *No blood.* The words continued to echo in his head, clamoring to the point of making him wince against them. Volkard stepped back from the boy. Muscles unclenched. Anger ebbed. To fulfill Marcellus' prophecy, he needed to get away from —everyone.

Volkard scooped up his wooden rudus and moved to the bare logs sunk deep in the ground standing like sentinels. In the constant rhythm of his early days of training, he whacked the practice sword against the training pole. *Thwack. Thwack. Thwack.* Strike after strike. Again and again, without thought or pause, he beat the stump. Driving the anger, the loss, the heartache from him. He couldn't stop until it was gone. Again. Again. Free himself of this hate. Of the blood lust that threatened to consume him.

Noting a blister at the base of his palm, he switched hands and continued assaulting the post with a relentless fervor. He could do this. He would be free of this fire consuming him.

"Germanicus?"

"What?" he shot back.

"Meal break."

"Not hungry."

A trainer stood before him, and Volkard raised his gaze to see the man who stood with his arms crossed. His expression held no anger or frustration. "I know, friend. But you can't continue to take your frustration and loss out on that hunk of wood without some fuel in you. Come now. The stump will be here upon your return."

Volkard looked around the arena—not another soul remained save him and the trainer. He allowed his weapon to slip from his hand and moved toward the dining chamber.

A hand fell on his shoulder, "We do ourselves a disservice when we make friends—but what is a man to do in this lonely life?"

Volkard grunted agreement as he entered to force the food into him. He knew they would not allow him to go without eating a second time.

Dropping to his bed, hours after the end of the day, Volkard's arms still hummed from the abuse he had visited on the stump all day. He tried to relax, but his muscles voiced their discomfort long after he had left the arena. He tossed from side to side, but sleep continued to hover at the edge of his grasp. He rose with a huff and paced for an unknown amount of time before he returned to his bed where slumber finally visited him.

It was not uncommon to see the one he still could not name visit him in his dreams. *She* would come to him with a smile. But this time was different. She stood at a distance; her countenance downcast. She turned and walked away.

"Wait! Don't go!" Volkard tried to follow, but figures as black as night seized hold of him. They prevented any forward movement. They pulled him down holding him flat against the ground by his ankles and wrists. Though the shadow forms were but vapors and wisps, he could not prevail against them. Twist and fight as he might, he only tired himself. A hand fell over his mouth and nose stopping the flow of air.

His body shook so violently a cut tore into his back from the rough ground beneath him. His chest burned, and his heart stuttered. With one hard wrench he freed his head. "Christus!"

Volkard own shout woke him. He sat straight up panting for breath. The breeze drifting through the window cooled his damp skin. He shoved his hands through his wet, mussed hair and sprang to his feet. Blood lay smeared on his mat. Part of the latticework holding the mat had broken and poked through cutting his back. Jerking his tunic from the back of the chair he yanked it over his head as he slipped out of his room.

Volkard lost count of the times he raced around the outer ring of the arena. His dream haunted him. Christus had banished the evil and helped him when he called. The knowledge shook him to the core. It drove out all thought save a smattering of memories. Marcellus' voice mingled with *hers*, creating a chorus in his head.

"Christus loves you."

"He seeks you."

"God has a purpose for you, Volkard."

"You will walk out of these walls and no blood will be on your hands."

He staggered to an open area and dropped to his knees in the sand. "God, Father of Christus, I know You are the only true God. There is no other like You. But Marcellus said I must confess all my sins to You." His gaze fell to his upturned palms resting on his knees. "How do I speak of the blood coating these hands? Kills from battles in the defense of my own and of myself, You could surely forgive. But the innocents, Christus—so many guiltless have fallen by these hands. A fury rages in my blood—and my hands are covered in their lifeblood. Still I can see the stains."

"His grace is sufficient for you."

Volkard tried to remember Marcellus saying those words.

"Will You forgive me—even all this, Christus?"

"If He can't forgive your sins, brother, then neither am I forgiven."

Those were Marcellus' last words of instruction to him. He raised his gaze to the star-filled sky along with his hands. "I confess all to You, Christus. All I did in killing so many. All the evil in my heart. Take it and make it new as Marcellus said. I choose to follow You. Do with me as You will."

A rush in his spirit—a stirring more powerful than any whirling wind followed Volkard's whispered words. The love they carried stole his breath and brought a song to his heart. Tears slid from his eyes as gratitude prostrate him before his God. His God. The thought danced in his mind. A God who loved him. Now Volkard understood why Marcellus was so eager to meet Him.

After a time of pure worship, Volkard rose and moved back toward the barracks—ready to sleep well for the last few hours before dawn.

"The bathing chambers are open if you wish to use them."

Volkard startled to see a trainer leaning against the wall relaxed as it he slept, though his eyes followed him with an alert gaze.

As he turned to the bathing chambers, Volkard realized he didn't care what the man had seen or what he thought. Because of the hatred the Romans harbored for all followers of the Way, he knew the man could have him killed. But he would trust his newfound Savior—in this life and the next.

CHAPTER

THIRTY

After a dip in the warm caldarium, Volkard enjoyed the deepest, sweetest sleep he could remember since being a babe in his mother's arms.

He rose the next morning a different man—from the inside out. He ate a hearty breakfast and trained as well as a gladiator should. And he waited. He believed Marcellus' words with all his heart. One day he would walk out of the gladiator school a free man.

Day followed day, and week followed week. Nothing changed. Laying on his bed looking through the high window another message came from his memory. "If we are still here, there must be a purpose."

"Christus, do you have a purpose in keeping me here? Is there something I should be doing?" Volkard resolved in his heart to keep a close watch for… what he didn't know.

But he didn't have a desire to speak at all. Not to the trainers—the novices, or any of the gladiators. He found nothing of interest in this life or in this place. But a joy bubbled in him—and there, in that sweetness, he was content. Nothing pressed on him other than to draw near to his God. Three months passed and Volkard knew no other companionship than that of his Savior.

"Welcome, my prized gladiators," Master Arturos said to the few men gathered around his table. "Tomorrow you fight for the honor of my school. Tonight, take your ease. Enjoy the food and the women." Arturos' hand waved out and women swept into the room—two for each man.

Volkard did as before and only answered questions with the briefest words possible.

The women ran their hands over his body, but their advances did not stir him. Looking up, he was sure he saw a vision of *her*. Her dark hair blew in a breeze he only felt in his spirit. And *she* smiled—oh how *she* smiled at him. These women throwing themselves at him could not compare with the one matchless woman who still held his heart.

"Germanicus, do you not care for my favors?" Arturos asked as he lounged on an elbow while a woman half his age fed him.

"I am grateful for all your kindnesses, Master."

"But you do not show your little birds any attention. Can I provide you another?"

"No Master. The only one I desire no longer draws breath. But I will see her again someday."

"Really?"

Volkard opened his mouth to speak, but the evening's entertainment arrived at that moment, and the fawning women beside him left to find more attentive men. He sat alone and quiet against a back wall.

As they left the master's home, Arturos placed his hand on

Volkard's shoulder. "You are my primus palus, Germanicus. As my top gladiator, I have bet on your victory. Do not disappoint me."

"I will not die in the arena. This I can promise you, Master."

"Good, good." He patted his shoulder and sent him to a goodnight's sleep.

As the gladiators battled and the crowd cheered, Volkard prayed. *Christus, I place my life in Your hands and trust in the promise Marcellus spoke over me. Let there never again be innocent blood on my hands. My God, show me a way to honor You even in this battle.*

"Germanicus, Thracian, Belen, enter the ring," the trainer said.

Three identically heavily armored fighters—not a usual match, but Volkard moved to the arena and wondered at the cheers for him above the others. Belen and he had met with neither prevailing last time. Thracian met them as a novice, his first time in combat.

Christus, I know how to come to a draw against one… but two? His mind tumbled back to one of many times his hands were covered in blood. He pushed the notion aside as the two men faced off against him. *I will not kill either, Lord. And if You require my life of me this day, I wait anxiously to see You soon—face to face.*

The matter settled within him, Volkard stood more relaxed than the other two and waited for them to make the first move. Thracian, showed his inexperience by stepping close to Belen as the novice took a large swing at Volkard.

Belen took advantage of Thracian's exposed rib cage and thrust his sword toward it.

Volkard brought his blade up from below blocking Thracian's large swing. At the same time Volkard's shoulder connected with

Belen's chest knocking him away from Thracian in the process and preventing the younger man's death. *Thank you, Lord.*

Thracian stumbled back at the near miss leaving Belen and Volkard to spar without him for a string of blows. The clanging of their swords rang in Volkard's ears even above the cheers of the crowd. Though Volkard saw opportunities, he never pressed them. Taking blow after blow—never giving ground and never taking it.

Pivoting so he could see Thracian better, Volkard continued to fight. Sharp small thrusts, the zing of honed blade edges sliding together. Thracian didn't move. Cowardice was a mortal sin in the arena.

Lord, show me a way to save him yet.

Belen lunged at Volkard, who spun away putting Thracian at his back. Volkard waited until Belen challenged him again. Grabbing hold of the man as he charged forward, Volkard turned him around and slammed Belen's back into Thracian's front. As both men sprang apart, Volkard went after Thracian, challenging him with familiar swings used in training.

Thracian responded, countering each blow as he had been taught. His arms knew what to do by instinct and long hours in the practice arena.

Belen tried to attack Volkard from behind but, standing sideways between them, he used his shield in defense against Belen and his sword to press Thracian. His shield arm now tired, Volkard flicked the tip of his sword, opening a small cut in Thracian's arm. The man pulled back out of instinct, giving Volkard time to turn the other direction. Now he met Belen blade to blade and defended against Thracian, who was not as fierce against his shield.

At some point Thracian turned his attention toward Belen combining his efforts with Volkard's. The two of them pressed Belen and worked him toward a wall, until Volkard succeeded in getting his foot tangled with Thracian causing him to trip into Belen' shield arm. All three men fell, more cuts were opened, but none grievous, and they were soon on their feet.

They battled two against one and one on one. Volkard saw opportunities again and again, but would not strike out to end either's life. He feigned a trip, changed opponents, and used his focused strikes to block one man's fatal blow against the other.

The stalemate continued double the length of his first match with Belen. Sweat dripped from them.

The crowd grew hoarse with its shouts.

Volkard thanked the Lord for the day of pounding the post using both arms—for now he could endure the beating each man dealt him.

At last the patron of this game, a senator of low ranking, called an end.

The three men stepped apart, and acknowledged him. Volkard's arms dangled limp at his sides, and he panted to bring the cooler air into his burning lungs.

Thank You, my Savior, Volkard prayed as he staggered to the gladiator chamber at the side of the arena. Stripped of weapons and armor, they returned to the ludus.

"Germanicus!"

Volkard turned at the master's sharp bark of his fighting name. His owner stood with several of the trainers, and he obediently moved toward them as the rest of the gladiators entered the baths.

He dared a glance after them, surprised at how much he would miss the cold waters of the frigidarium.

As he stood before Arturos, the trainers surrounded him. Ennius, the man who most often trained him stood with his arms crossed—as always—but a pleading gaze fell from his eyes.

"You failed me!" Arturos screamed in his face.

CHAPTER

THIRTY-ONE

Surrounded by all the trainers and facing the wrath of his owner, Volkard did not flinch or raise his voice. "I did as I promised, Master."

Wham! A fist flew, pounding into his jaw.

Volkard licked the blood from his lip. The familiar metallic taste gave him an odd sense of comfort. "I promised not to die, and here I—"

Two more blows came—each from opposite sides—snapping his head one way and then the other.

Volkard shook the ringing from his skull and brushed his forearm across his mouth.

"I bet on you to win. Placed a lot of money on the odds of my mighty German Barbarian to kill two at once."

Volkard remained silent.

"I know why the fire has gone out of you. Why you no longer fight with the ferocity I saw in you in the beginning."

Standing still, his eyes on Arturos' feet, Volkard waited. *No matter the power of this man on earth, I know my life rests in Your hands. Your will be done, Christus.* Though new to his faith, his trust was complete. Once he made his decision, Volkard would not be moved from it. His God had met him in every way. Now, he would stand firm in the truth he felt in his entire body.

"You have turned from your worship of the war gods and now follow the Jewish traitor. The one they call Christus. You are a follower of the Way. Do you deny it?"

Volkard raised his head to meet the man's gaze. He knew the consequences of being a follower of Christus in the Roman world. But it didn't matter. "No, I do not deny it. I follow Christus."

All five of the trainers around him took turns throwing punches to his face, ribs, and gut.

Volkard fought to regain his breath and remain standing.

"A death sentence is ordered to all the followers of the dead Jew called Jesus. I ask you again, are you a follower of the Way? Of this Christus?"

Volkard widened his stance, placed his hands behind his back, and held the master's hard stare. "I know the cost, but I tell you, I am—now and forever—a faithful follower of Christus."

Fists pounded every part of his body as Arturos walked away. No longer able to stand, Volkard he dropped to the ground where their fists were joined by kicks from their spike-covered caligae. The nails on the soles ripped deep into his flesh as bones shattered.

"I commit my spirit to my God."

Cool air. Agonizing pain.

A groan rattled through his broken body adding to his torment.

A thick bitter liquid poured over his tongue.

Searing pain.

His own scream rattled his shattered body.

More of the thick, bitter liquid.

While Volkard quaked with violent trembling in the coolness surrounding him, he burned with raging heat from within.

A wet cloth brushed his face, chest, arms and legs.

Bitter liquid.

Muttered voices. Echoes of hollow drips. Smoke. Unending pain.

He tried to open his eyes, but only one cracked open. Faint flickering light did little to push away the deep shadows. His heart pounded steadily in his head and against his damaged ribs. Breaths were shallow.

A hand held a cup to his lips. More disgusting liquid.

"How long?" Volkard croaked at the shadow tending the fire. Lying flat on his back both arms and legs bound and stiff. He could not move more than his head.

"Almost a month," the shadow said. "Drink. Rest. You may yet live."

One eye fully open, the other almost. He turned to the sound of the voices. "Master?"

Arturos came and stood over him. "You are the first. I have had others come through my school—followers of this subversive

God. But none have had the courage to say as much. Most have been like your companion. They purposely die in the arena to meet this God of theirs."

He squatted beside Volkard holding him in a steely stare. "But you did not do that either. You fought hard—but only to a draw and no further. You are an odd one Germanicus. Not the blood thirsty barbarian I'd hoped for over a year ago."

Arturos gripped Volkard's chin in his hand, sending bolts of fresh pain through his body. "You have changed, Germanicus, and I will know how. You will teach me all the ways of these Christians. As long as you draw breath, I have hired this physician, Ovid, to tend to your wounds here in this cave below my school. When I am satisfied I know all about the disruptive cult, I may choose to grant you freedom." He stood. "But know this, everyone believes you are dead. I can make that a reality at any moment of my choosing. Do you understand these conditions?"

"Yes, Master."

Arturos turned and walked across the cavern in which Volkard lay.

The warmth of God filled him with energy he did not possess. "Master?"

The man stopped and glanced over his shoulder at him.

"Christus loves you. He died for you."

CHAPTER

THIRTY-TWO

Time passed unmarked due to the lack of natural light in the cave. Ovid removed the first of his splints from Volkard's left arm. The physician also helped him to sit for short spells each day.

"Are you prepared to begin, Germanicus?" Arturos materialized from the darkness and sat on a cushioned stool he placed near Volkard.

Volkard swallowed, nearly choking on his unease. He prayed he would remember Marcellus' words, that he would say them correctly to express the truth of this faith that met his every need. Give him a sword and point him at any enemy and he would charge headlong against him. But talk about a God he had just met himself? Could he do that? *Fill my mouth with Your words, my Savior.* Volkard opened his lips, and a message not his own washed over his tongue. "I am honored to teach you in the ways of my God. I will begin where Marcellus began instructing me—at the beginning." Everything Marcellus had ever said to him leapt back to the forefront of his mind. He smiled. God would do this; he only needed to open his mouth.

Arturos sat with his arms crossed. "It seems like a reasonable place."

"In the beginning the world was void and there was nothing until God spoke it into—"

Arturos shot to his feet upsetting the stool. "You don't seriously expect me to keep you alive as you recite all of history?"

"Without the beginning, you will not understand why Christus, the one named Jesus, came to die a Roman traitor's death."

The master paced, arms crossed tight. He turned to leave, stopped and spun back around. "Very well, but if this is a ploy to live longer, it will only serve to hasten your death." He righted the stool and landed on it with a *harrumph*.

"It matters not what I say, or what you do, Arturos. My life is in my Savior's hands—not yours." Volkard chose to address his superior by his given name. It was dangerous—but he placed his hope in the Lord. He wanted to speak man to man—not slave to master. As a friend and—with God's grace—a soon to be brother.

Arturos drew his sword leveling at it Volkard's throat. "I beg to differ."

Volkard smiled. "If you kill me, you release me from this constant pain and send me to my beloved God. There I will live for eternity without pain, tears, or suffering. I welcome that journey." Volkard raised his chin to give the man a better target. Peace flooded him, for live or die, he trusted Christus to be with him.

The sword disappeared into its sheath once more. "Speak man, while you yet draw breath."

Volkard lowered his head, his eyes closed in a brief moment of disappointment at not being with his Savior. He again heard his friend's words. "You will walk from this place a free man…" *Yes,*

Marcellus, I still remember your promise spoken over me. And I know that if I yet draw breath, it is for some divine reason.

He opened his eyes and looked on Arturos. Volkard smiled. "So, the world was void until God spoke everything into existence. The finest of His creation was man. Man and woman were placed in a garden with only one restriction. Do not eat of the Tree of Knowledge of Good and Evil. But they ate and their eyes were opened—"

"I do not understand your God. If He is indeed all powerful why would He not protect the tree or remove it from where they could get to it?" The master's voice dripped with disdain.

"Man is given free will. We choose whether we will follow God or reject Him."

Arturos' brows drew together, his lips twisted into a scowl.

"You have a wife and children, do you not, Arturos."

The master gave a curt nod.

"Tell me, do they love you?"

"Well, of course they do! What are you getting at Germanicus? I am a good husband and father. I provide well for them."

"But do you not force them to love you, do you? No spell of the ancient gods was spoken over them? They have not been threatened into showing you love?"

"Of course not!"

Volkard smiled. "And because they give you love freely, is it not more precious, more cherished? Would it not be cheap and of little value were it not given from a free will?"

Arturos conceded with a silent nod.

"Such is the same with God Almighty. He could have forced us to love Him, but He wants us to choose Him—even over our own lives. So, He allowed the first of our kind to choose to disobey—and thus sin entered the world. Every man and woman who followed them is born with this sinful nature. All except Jesus, the Christus. We cannot escape it. Every inclination of the heart of man is evil all the time. It matters not who we are—we have all failed to live up to God's perfect standard. Even a tiny drop of blood will ruin a lovely toga."

"I am a good man. I provide for my family. I am an honorable Roman citizen. I treat my gladiators well." Arturos rattled his list of good deeds.

"But are you a perfect man? Have you never told an untruth? Cheated on a few coins owed to Caesar? Allowed your eyes and thoughts to stray to a lovely woman?"

Arturos stood abruptly. "That will be enough for today, Germanicus." He disappeared into the dark as silently as he had entered.

Volkard looked to Ovid. The man faced away from him and ground herbs to make a tea that would allow Volkard a few hours of pain-free sleep. Bowing his head, Volkard sought his God. "Thank you, Lord, for this opportunity to speak of You to this powerful Roman. May You continue to give me the words each time he comes that he needs to hear. May Arturos not stop visiting me until he gives his life to You."

Would Arturos give his life to Christus? Was that really the reason Volkard languished in the stone prison? One more soul won? Or was there another reason? Something Volkard had yet to uncover?

CHAPTER

THIRTY-THREE

Arturos didn't return for a couple of weeks. And when he did, he was in a bad-temper as he again took his place on the stool beside Volkard.

"I like not at all the way your words disturb me, Germanicus. Since last I was here, I have thought of nothing else but the ills I have done the whole of my life."

Volkard could not suppress his smile. "May I ask, has any other god, or emperor ever affected you in like manner? Showed you your shortcomings and made you want to change?"

"No." Arturos growled, and the corner of his lip curled in a vicious snarl.

"How do you account for the difference now?"

The man did not respond.

Volkard answered for him. "There is power and truth in the words spoken in the name of Christus. He is not like any other god you have ever known."

Arturos slammed his fist onto his thigh. "So how do I stop feeling this way?"

"Ah, there is only one thing you can do—accept what Christus has done for you and allow Him to rule your life."

"I will not surrender to the enemy of Rome. I will not become a hated follower of the Way. This Christus asks too much." Arturos stormed off, this time the echoes of his sandals slapping the stone marked his passing.

Only a week passed before he returned, his face downcast and his eyes red with dark circles beneath. "If I kill you and release you to this paradise you love, will your God let me alone?"

"The Creator of the universe is ever patient," Volkard chuckled. "If He wishes you to be one of His own—and He died on the cross to assure you could be—He will not stop pursuing you until He has you… even if you killed a thousand men."

Arturos rocked back on his stool, his eyes wide. "Your perfect God could forgive me such grievous sins?"

Volkard held his gaze with a hard stare. He held out his hands before the man. "I have killed many, Arturos. More than my soul can bear—soldiers, enemies, and the innocent. Their blood stained my hands until I no longer saw flesh but only gore. Christus paid my debt for all those lives. I stand cleansed and pure before God my Father as if I never sinned."

Arturos stared at the hands, "But He just asks so much in return." Today his dragging feet slid into the darkness.

From that day on, Arturos came every day. He listened in near silence to all Volkard told him as Volkard marveled at the words flowing so freely from his lips. Had he really attended Marcellus' teaching so well? Or had God etched the lessons in his heart for such a time as this? Each visit saw Volkard stronger and more healed, and he lost count of the days they spent together in deep study of the One True God.

In the early morning hours, and in the evenings after Arturos returned to his family, Volkard moved about on mended limbs. He stretched and worked to increase his strength and flexibility. He used the many stones scattered about to build up his strength. Pushing the smaller ones in the beginning, then lifting them, and once he could accomplish these tasks with ease, he moved to the larger stones and worked with them.

Ovid, the man tasked with his healing, marveled at his recovery. "You heal better and faster than any man I have ever treated," his chest puffed up.

"Though I appreciate your fine efforts, Ovid, I must tell you, it is my God who restores me."

A frown pulled on the man's face. "You are so sure of this?" Volkard nodded.

A smirk came to the lean man's lips. "And what happens when Master Arturos returns and slits your throat."

Volkard approached him and sat the good sized bolder he carried at the man's feet and rested against it. He looked straight into Ovid's eyes. "I have been assured I will leave here alive."

Ovid crossed his arms. "Master Arturos has never spoken those words."

"No," Volkard conceded with a shake of his head. "My God did."

Ovid's mouth hung open, but no words came. Volkard rose, patted the physician's shoulder, and returned to his own private training.

Day after day as Arturos came, Ovid sat with his back to them making ointments, bandages, or notes on his scroll, but his head always leaned toward the conversation behind him as Volkard spoke of the promises of Christus who came for all men.

Volkard hoisted rocks over his head waiting for Arturos. Eventually his friend arrived, and they sat and talked of God.

"You were saying yesterday that Christus was seen after He died and was buried in the tomb."

"It is true. Many of the Savior's disciplines saw Him in the days that followed."

"There was gossip at the time that the body had been stolen. Some said the guards were derelict in their duties."

"You do not sound as though you believe that."

"Even when I first heard it I could not truly believe those guards would neglect their duty—not one so important especially since they feared the man's followers would attempt such a thing. Months later, I learned that the guards where paid off by the emperor and living well in another part of the empire. One of the guard's cousins worked for me for a time. He swore both his cousin and the other guards with him never slept or left their post. The stone moved of its own, and the body was gone. But the money? Why pay them if they had failed at such a critical task? They deserved death."

"Why indeed?" Volkard smiled and left the question hanging between them.

Volkard moved from lifting rocks to climbing them, building

strength in his legs as well as his arms.

Arturos entered carrying a bag in his hand. He greeted Volkard with a firm handshake and a smirking smile. "The time has come, Germanicus."

Volkard raised a brow in question.

"Today I free you. I can't, in good conscience, leave a brother here in the dark any longer while I take my family to a safer region of the empire."

"Brother?"

"Oh, must I even admit the words to you?"

"Remember I told you God said, 'If you deny Me before men, I will deny you before the Father,'" Volkard said.

"Yes, I have accepted Christus and His rule in my life. Are you satisfied? You and your persistent God are the victors over me—and my entire family."

Volkard reached out and embraced the man. "To God alone be the glory. Great things He has done."

Arturos cleared his throat and Volkard released him. "I know He has done great things, but I feel led to take my family away from the city. Christians are not safe here." He reached out the bag toward Volkard. "I have freed you. You will find all the appropriate documents to prove you are a respected citizen of the Roman Empire—but it is even more dangerous for you in this city, Germa—Volkard." He corrected himself using Volkard's given name for the first time. "Many have seen you fight in the arena and those still in the ludus believe you dead. You have spent over half a year healing down here, but they will remember you." He led Volkard in the opposite direction he usually left.

"What of Ovid? I have not seen him in many days."

Arturos' hand came to rest on Volkard's shoulder. "Our God has claimed him as well. He asked for leave to go and spread the good news where he may as he practices his healing craft. He hopes to mend both body and soul." A joyful laugh bubbled up from deep within Arturos.

Around several twists and turns, daylight lit a narrow entrance. "This will lead you outside behind the ludus. It is not a populated area of the city, but people are always about. Wait until deep night and use the cloak," he pointed to the bag in Volkard's hand, "to conceal yourself. Make haste in any direction away from here."

Volkard reached out his hand and let a ray of sun fall across his pale arm. Warmth travelled up spreading across his shoulders and added strength to the peace within him.

"I wager you never thought you would see this day."

Volkard laughed so boisterously he covered his mouth to keep the sound from drawing unwanted attention from outside. "I knew from the day I entered your care, I would one day walk from here a free man and there would be no blood on my hands."

"Marcellus' prophecy?"

Volkard only nodded. "And the day you came railing about the stirring our God was doing in your heart, I knew you would one day surrender to Him." Volkard's hand fell onto Arturos' shoulder now. "I am truly grateful you are not as hardheaded as I, my brother. For I would have been white like a marble statue when I left, if you took as long as I did to surrender to His will."

The men laughed for a moment.

Arturos' gaze moved to the light. "Do you know where you

will go, Volkard?"

Following the shorter man's gaze, Volkard looked far beyond the cave walls into the unseen distance. "North. I don't know where for sure, but I am drawn to go back the way I came. Perhaps the good Lord wishes me to return to my own people and teach them as I have you. Or perhaps He has something different in mind for my life." He drew in a long slow breath and brushed away the pain rising afresh within him. "There is one I lost. One dear to me far more than I dared believe. One whose name I cannot speak without tearing my very heart from my chest. I will go to the place of her death and tell her I now follow her God. And say good-bye."

He shook the grief from his shoulders with a toss of his head and turned to Arturos' extended hand. "And you brother, where do you head with your family?"

The men grasped forearms. "I hear tell there is a faithful group of Christians yet in Ephesus. We go there to see the truth of the matter."

"I pray Godspeed and protection go with you wherever you travel, and I will see you again in glory, my brother."

"Godspeed, protection, and comfort to you as well, Volkard."

Arturos left him leaning against the wall waiting for nightfall.

CHAPTER

THIRTY-FOUR

Footfalls approached the opening and a shadow block the bright sunlight streaming through the opening. The footsteps quickly faded as whoever passed outside continued on his way. Volkard drew in a steadying breath and swiped the sweat from his brow. When was the last time he felt so hot? Maybe the fever after he arrived in the cave? However, with the perceived threat passed, the cool air again washed over his skin.

His hand still shook though as he reached for the bag Arturos left him. Fear captured his heart. He relived each punch and kick he received to get hidden away in this pit. Volkard had feared few men since leaving his homeland to make a way for himself. Now he felt like that boy in his village as the raiders attacked.

Dropping the bag, he bent a knee. "God, Arturos spoke truth. There is great danger for me outside this cave. Don't leave me now…" His words faltered as Marcellus' teachings came fresh to his mind. God went with him. Volkard rocked back on his heels. God was with him *now*. Another steadying breath filled his lungs. His heart rate slowed. A smile pulled at his lips. "Lead, and I will follow."

Volkard reached into the bag, pulled out a clean, light brown linen tunic and an expansive length of fabric for his toga. He spent much of the day arranging the draped garment in the style he had seen Romans wear but with limited success. There must be some trick fathers taught their sons before they reached majority, for it was not a simple matter to form the graceful drape of the fabric that looked so effortless on all Rome's citizens.

"Good enough," he grumbled in German. It had been long since his native tongue fell from his lips, and it had an odd sensation rolling around his mouth.

Next, Volkard pulled a leather pouch of coins from the bag. The weight of them sat heavy in his hand, and he fingered the pouch making the coins clink together. Surely his former master had left him with more money than Arturos had paid to bring Volkard to the ludus. "What purpose might You have for this, my Lord?" he asked switching back to Latin without thought.

Securing the pouch inside the toga fabric on a belt around his tunic, Volkard turned to the final items in the bag. The documents Arturos had promised—though Volkard couldn't read them, a short red cloak with a hood, two loaves of bread, a wedge of cheese, and a gladius sat in his hands. Laying the food, scroll, and cloak aside, he drew the sword from its sheath as a late afternoon ray of sun filtered into the entrance. The honed edge caught the light casting reflections on all the walls around him. A shudder stampeded down his spine. He forced the weapon back into its leather shroud and dropped it to the ground.

He waited until his breathing once again calmed. Being careful of his toga, he turned his back on the weapon again kneeling in the dust. "Lord God Almighty, I refuse to return to the man of blood I once was. No longer will I bear a sword against friend or enemy. I place my life into Your hands alone." He stood, arranged the toga yet again, and glanced down at the sword. "Never again," he vowed through clenched teeth.

Volkard took his first steps toward the open space outside the cave about an hour after dark. The slap of leather on the stone road outside drove him back away from the opening.

He waited what he believed was a couple more hours before he attempted to exit again, but sounds once more sent him shrinking into the shadows.

I have not given you a spirit of fear.

He startled at the voice that was not a voice. It came from nowhere and everywhere at the same time.

I have not given you a spirit of fear, but one of power, love, and self-discipline.

"Yes, my Lord. I go. Lead me where Your will wishes." With bold steps, Volkard walked out into an empty street under a starry night. A quick glance to the heavens gave him his bearing, and he turned north and walked. The wind ruffled the toga, the fabric flapping against him—its coolness raising bumps on his flesh. He pulled the cloak about him and raised the hood.

Long before daybreak, Volkard strolled through the open gate with only a brief glance from the soldiers standing nearby. He placed one foot in front of the other in even steps until he was well beyond the sight of the city.

His freedom played in his soul. Laughter bubbled in his throat. His feet fairly danced along the hard-packed Roman road. The sun rose on his right, smiling its good pleasure on him adding to his joy.

"Hand over your coin!"

Volkard's feet stumbled, and he came up short in a lurching fashion as four sword-wielding men materialized around him. By instinct, his hand reached for his own weapon, but it grasped nothing. Volkard smiled. *I am Yours, my Lord. You said I would walk a free man from Roman captivity. But You never promised how far I would travel.*

"The coins."

Volkard raised his hands, the smile still dancing on his lips. "I have nothing to give you." He didn't lie. He had no intention of turning over Arturos' coins. Why? He didn't know.

"Search him," the one talking whisked his blade tip toward another. As the second man stepped near, Volkard noted how small they all were compared to him. None reached his chin in height nor did any outweigh him. Volkard stepped back from the newcomer as possibilities rattled around in his head. He could easily pick the man up and throw him into at least two of his fellow thieves. He could snap his neck as he had dispatched the weasel-man who betrayed the Sanctuary. He was the last man Volkard had killed—two years ago. Sword or no, he vowed to God not to be that man any longer. He took another step back.

A sword tip pressed against his shoulder. He held his arms out straight at his side as the approaching man ran his hands around him searching for anything of value.

Arturos' sack carrying his food was tossed to one of the others to search.

The man searching him turned to their leader who had given the order. "There's nothing on him."

How had he missed it? The purse of coins sat tucked under his belt, but surely he would have noted the bulge. Peace and joy coursed through him. God had kept it hidden.

"All he has is a little food." Another grumbled, tossing it into a ditch.

"Beat him," the first man ordered.

"What goes on here?"

Before a fist could fly, Volkard raised his gaze to see a small band of Roman soldiers coming around the next bend.

The bandits looked startled and stood rooted in place.

"The thieves we have been searching for, sir," a soldier pointed with a shout.

The thieves darted in opposite directions, and the soldiers gave chase. In but a moment, Volkard again stood on the empty road. He blinked, let his hand slide down his side, and found the coin pouch the man had missed. The mirth returned to his lips and danced about his insides. He sang praises to the Lord as he retrieved his food sack and continued north. How would God show Himself next? Volkard couldn't wait to find out.

CHAPTER

THIRTY-FIVE

Volkard divided up his coins after the run-in with the thieves on the road. When he arrived in the next city, he purchased a few things he needed including a bedroll and a small dagger to cut his food. He went to the northern gate and waited. He hoped to follow along with a group of traveling merchants who were also heading north. Finding such a caravan not long after midday, he followed. Not so close as to make them nervous and not so far as to be singled out as a lone traveler.

The night air cooled driving away the warmth of the day as the merchants turned off to stay in an inn along the road. Volkard moved to the tree line, threw out his roll, and ate of his rations. "Thank you, Lord, for Your protection, Your care, and Your faithfulness. Lead me and I shall follow."

He settled on his back with his arm behind his head staring up at the stars. "Tell *her* I miss her," he whispered.

He slept later than he had planned. The first day and part of the night he had walked without stopping. His legs were tight and complained of being overworked. Volkard ate and waited for the next caravan of travelers heading his way.

And thus, he traveled, with others—but not. Stopping in cities only long enough to replenish his food stores and wait for the next band to follow. And he never ceased to find something to thank his God for providing. "Thank You for the fine weather in which to travel. Thank You for the kindness of the woman who offered me one of her sweet cakes. Thank You for the freedom to walk this road at my leisure unhindered by chains."

Waking one morning among the trees he stood and stretched. "Every day I ache less and cover more ground. Thank You, Christus." He rolled his mat and slipped it over his shoulder. "Might I know where we are going?"

The breeze rustled the leaves around him pulling them north.

"Yes, north," Volkard smiled.

Entering one walled city, a cohort of soldiers marched straight at him. Those in the front ranks shouted orders Volkard barely heard over the thumping of his heart. He stepped out of their path as did everyone else. The soldiers brandished weapons at a few who didn't move fast enough. Women yelped, grabbing for children, as Volkard's eyes locked with one of the soldiers. Those eyes were burned into his memory. This was the one who had ordered the Sanctuary's common building set on fire.

Hot rage and icy fear collided in his chest. Volkard's feet grew roots and anchored him where he stood.

The solider stared, but recognition never showed on his face. He blinked, looked away, and kept marching past.

As the last of the rank passed by, a breath slipped from Volkard, and he staggered back a step almost bumping into a mother who consoled her frightened child.

"They are gone now, my love. We are safe. They will not hurt us."

The words were spoken by the woman to her child, but they came from his God straight to Volkard's heart. Again, his God had saved him.

He lost count of the days he walked, or the cities he passed through, checking now and then for direction from God and never getting more than for him to continue the way he was headed. Away from the larger cities, Volkard abandoned the noble toga and changed to a tunic and long, lose-fitting trousers—still with the hated Roman sandals. As his journey moved farther north into the cooler lands, he also purchased a warmer cloak.

At a bend in the road, he lost sight of the cart with the clanking pots he had followed. An inn caught his eye on his right. At first, he thought nothing of it as he had passed many on his journey thus far. But there was something familiar about the curve along the road and where the inn sat beside it. The noise of the pot merchant's cart became a distant clinking as Volkard's footsteps faltered.

The inn's door hung loose on its hinges. Weeds grew all about. One post for holding up the awning lay broken making the corner of its roof sag. Shutters lay on the ground.

Volkard braced himself on his knees willing his sickening stomach to be still. His eyes traced off to where the soldiers had thrown the body of the weasel—the last man he had killed. This was the inn Volkard had come to with *her*. The one where they almost spoke freely with one another and the weasel translated. The one where they hid from the soldiers before escaping into the hills where they believed they would be safe.

Volkard leaned a shaking hand against a tree and looked in the direction where he had last seen *her* on that day the soldiers came to destroy all he held dear. He doubled over and retched.

Wiping his mouth on his sleeve, he looked to the heavens. Dusk revealed little between the many branches. "Father, why am I here?"

The door banged against its frame in a small gust of wind.

"No one is here anymore." Volkard stared at the structure unable to move to it or past it.

Volkard's thoughts tumbled around as though tossed in a violent storm. Suddenly a voice broke through the uproar.

"It is a shame someone does not rebuild that place. It was always far better than anything in the town beyond."

Volkard glanced up at the man riding past on a weary pony. The rider nodded at Volkard and continued on his way.

"Rebuild it, Christus?" He staggered back into the tree until it supported his full weight—his back pressed hard against it. "You want me here?" He shook his head. "I cannot do it. Lord, please. I cannot look out my front door and see the place where she lies cold in the ground every day."

He panted for breath around the lump of dread lodged in his throat. His legs threatened to drop him to the dusty road. A small drizzle wet his cheeks. *I will go where You lead.* His own words echoed back in the growing storm mocking him.

"Lord, give me strength."

CHAPTER

THIRTY-SIX

Volkard moved across the road on wobbly legs. He pulled the dangling door out of the way and stepped inside the inn. The air sat heavy and almost foul in the first open room. For a moment he was sure he saw a vision of her sitting there at the table talking with him from two years ago. He lurched outside, shaking. "*She* is not here. *She* was taken from me on the mountainside. I cannot bear to be in this place without *her* now."

Warmth wrapped around him more firm than the ground he stood upon and deeper than the cave he'd recovered in. Peace and comfort came in waves lapping against his aching spirit. After a time, he turned and walked inside again. The room lay empty except a few broken furniture legs and scattered forest debris blown in through the decrepit door and open windows.

He walked through the first room. It held memories of her. There was a small hallway beyond that led into sleeping chambers on the right and left and a kitchen space straight ahead. The door leading from the kitchen out into the field behind the inn was no longer there at all. Something moved beyond the doorway in the growing darkness.

Volkard froze, straining to hear who waited there. At last,

realizing no one was going to burst in on him with murderous intent, he crept out into the large clearing behind the inn. Next to a well, with several stones missing, was a lopsided trough; beside it stood the trembling form of a ghost of a donkey.

Its eyes bulged from its sunken face, and every bone poked from its body. Some cruel person had tethered the beast out here. In its hunt for food and water, the creature had thoroughly wound its lead around the obstacles in the yard. Now it didn't have enough freedom to lower its head to the last strands of grass.

It blinked at Volkard once.

Volkard shook his head. "Well you have gotten yourself in quite a fix." He approached the beast with slow quiet steps and drew the small dagger he used for meals from his belt. As he lifted it toward the donkey, Volkard considered slitting the poor creature's throat and putting it out of its misery. But he couldn't even kill this dumb animal. He cut through the lead releasing it.

Next, Volkard moved to the well and, after replacing the rotted rope with some from his sack, he lowered an old bucket into the depths. The first few loads Volkard brought up were nothing more than leaves and twigs covering the surface. The subsequent several buckets came up full of brackish foul water, spoiled by the rotting forest debris. Finally, he brought up water that—at least for the donkey—would be drinkable.

He poured several buckets-full into the trough, and the donkey came and drank. It emptied all that Volkard had put in it and tossed its head with a weak bray for more.

"You are impatient. Keep your fur on, I'm moving as fast as I can."

After the creature had its fill it moved into the darkness and Volkard recognized the sounds of torn and munched grass.

Throwing out his bedroll, Volkard lay on the threshold of the kitchen, out of the rain that had started falling again as he finished with the donkey. Listening to the soft symphony of rain and wind, Volkard prayed. "Please, my God, may I leave this place?"

A soft nudged drew Volkard from his sleep. He rolled to his back but didn't open his eyes. A weight pushed into his middle and nipped and tugged at his shirt. Alertness surged through his limbs, and Volkard's eyes flew open. He stared up at a whisker-covered muzzle. The large scraggy head nudged him again. Volkard pushed it away.

The donkey threw back its head and brayed.

Volkard rubbed his face with his hands, trying to rid himself of the last remnants of sleep. "You mongrel, what do you want? The sun is barely up."

The creature nodded its head several times, then walked to the empty trough and brayed again.

Volkard stood, stretched, and moved out of the inn. The beast bellowed again. "Ow, but you are an impatient creature." He filled the trough and pulled up another bucket of water. He threw his hands in and splashed his face.

As Volkard leaned against the well, staring at the building, the donkey came and rubbed against his hand. Volkard absent-mindedly pet the creature. "You're welcome, Ol' Man." He sighed. "Lord, where to today?" He was no longer compelled to put one foot in front of the other. "Christus?" His heart shuddered in the silence.

After the sun crested the far hills and washed over him, Volkard groaned. "I will go to the place *she* died… I will say my apologies and be on my way." He took a stepped toward the door, but the donkey blocked his path. Volkard tried to go around the creature, but the donkey moved to the door and put a hoof on his bedroll blocking the doorway.

"What is the matter with you? Get out of the way."

The donkey stepped up into the building placing both front hooves on the roll and tossed his head.

"You can tell me no all you want, you mangy creature, but I am not staying here." Volkard went around the building and entered through the precariously attached front door. He aimed to shove the donkey off his mat and out the back door with a running start.

The foul odor in the first room assaulted him again, and his gaze caught on where he knew the trap door to be hidden in the floor. He stood over it, his stomach roiling. Grateful he hadn't eaten since mid-meal yesterday, he crouched and felt for the carved-out spot that would allow him to pull the hatch open. He found it but couldn't summon the courage to heave it up. A tremor raced over him. He knew what he would find. He inhaled, stood, and tossed back the trap door in one smooth motion.

He stumbled back covering his face with his forearm and swallowed the bitter wash at the back of his throat. Two bodies lay crumpled at the bottom. The dim morning light revealed white bone, sluffing flesh and tattered clothes. Volkard staggered out the backdoor past the donkey who followed him into the grass where he retched. The dry heaves echoed across the open field.

He sat back on his heels and gazed at a rise about half a mile away. The sun danced there, and he knew. He rummaged around the inn for something to dig with. Finding a scoop-shaped stone near the well, he walked out to the sight and started digging. It took him nearly all day to make a pit deep enough for what remained of the innkeeper and her mate.

In the waning light of the setting sun, Volkard finished a new ladder and grabbed a large remnant of cloth he found in one of the rooms. He tied a small piece around his nose and mouth and went down into the pit—now grave—where *she* and he had safely hidden from the soldiers.

He gagged as he moved the bodies onto the rest of the large cloth. Wiping the sweat from his brow with his forearm, he secured the corners of the cloth and pulled the bodies up and outside to the hole. He honored them by laying them out, and then covered them with dirt and prayed. "Lord, grant peace to those who offered peace to strangers, safety to those who gave safe passage, and kindness to those who were kind in Your name."

At the well, he yanked off his tunic and dumped a bucket of cold water over his head before he scrubbed the garment. He drained the trough after he was done, refilled it with water for the donkey, and draped his tunic over the well roof to dry. He dropped down on his bedroll. His muscles were tight, breathing labored, and stomach aching. Staring out at the stars, he listened to the donkey pad around and munch on grass. "May I go *now*, Lord?"

No answer came and he covered his face with his hands, tears burn the back of his eyes for the first time in two years.

CHAPTER

THIRTY-SEVEN

Laughter bubbled from the outer room as Volkard sliced a hunk of meat and arranged it on a platter. A smile danced on his lips. He carried the tray out into the large open room of the inn. A woven mat covered the trap door and five tables set atop it, each surrounded by chairs.

"Welcome," a melodious voice sang as the door swung open, and his heart thrilled at the sound. He turned but did not see the speaker as three more people entered.

The man arriving inclined his head as a woman holding a child's hand took a seat at the last table. "Have you a bed for tonight?"

"There is always room in the inn," Volkard heard himself say as he set the tray on another table and turned to his new guests. His heart floated in his chest. He could not remember a time he had known such joy—other than when his Savior had forgiven him. "Welcome, would you like something to eat?"

The man wrung his hands together. "We only have enough for the bed, sir."

Volkard noted their weary expression, the dust on their clothes and skin, the wear of their sandals. He smiled, and made a quick decision. "The price is the same for the food and the bed. Enjoy."

Plates were set before them and another tray of food appeared on their table. But Volkard hadn't done it. Someone was with him. The owner of the voice that stirred him earlier. Before he could turn to see his helper, the woman sat the child in his own chair, grasped Volkard's hand and whispered, "Christus bless you."

Volkard sat bolt upright startling the donkey who brayed his displeasure. Shaking his head to wash away the dream, Volkard rose on shaking legs and staggered to the well where he again splashed water on his face. Tossing back his head, he stared at the night sky. Dawn was still far off. Volkard dropped to sit by the well, his elbow on his knees, face in his hands. "Lord, You want me to open this place to Your children in need once more?"

A breeze caressed him, and God's good pleasure filled him.

"Oh, Lord," he moaned. "I am not strong enough to be so near the memories of *her*. Please take this burden from me."

The donkey plodded near and pressed his soft muzzle against Volkard's head. The creature nuzzled against him before it lay down and rested its head in his lap.

No sleep visited him for the remainder of the night, and as dawn lit the eastern sky, Volkard made his decision. If he wished to experience the joy of the vision, he had to be obedient. He looked at the back of the inn knowing the last owners had died for their work. But death no longer held a grip on him. He knew where he would go after his last breath, and he knew those who would meet him there. It was the one he was sure God planned to bring along side of him that made him shudder.

He nudged the donkey off him and rose to his feet. He pulled the soiled garment off the well. Grime covered it in light splotches, but he had nothing else to wear. His tunic would have to be replaced before he found the government official he needed to speak to about taking over the inn. Volkard rummaged through his belongings and found the last of the money Arturos had gifted him. Counting it out, his heart dared hope it would not be enough.

"Lord, if this truly is the only course for me, You will have to make it work with the meager coins I have left. I must pay for the privilege to own this place that breaks my heart, and I yet need materials to fix and fill it as well." He lifted the pouch to the heavens. "This is Yours, and I am Your servant. Your will be done."

Tucking the bag away, Volkard pulled out the length of fabric he used as a toga in the beginning and draped it over the tunic hoping it hid the worst of the stains and grime. No point in wasting any of the money God had entrusted to him. He stepped out and set the door in the frame so it closed the entryway and headed down the road. His gaze slipped up the steep rise on his left where he had last seen *her* before the fire. Pain, longing, and love threatened to steal his breath as it tighten around his chest and throat. He fought to take in a full breath. "I will keep my promise to come to *you* soon. Let us see what the Lord has for me this day first." He patted the donkey, "Be back soon, Ol' Man."

CHAPTER

THIRTY-EIGHT

Volkard walked through the gate back into the city where he had last been with *her* before the inn. He had followed *her* as a humble servant—and resented it. He knew she did it to protect him, and his love for *her* pricked at his wounded spirit once more. He passed through the square with all its vendors peddling their wares. The shop where she had drawn the fish symbol marking her as a Christian was now the booth of a jeweler. What happened to the former Christian owner? Had she been killed like the innkeepers? He shuddered at the thought.

He passed the place where they first stopped and where *she* had ordered a drink. It still served refreshments to customers. His stomach bellowed in protest of his neglect the last couple of days. He turned down another street trudging toward, what would account for, a forum in this small city. He would see what money he had left after his talk with the official.

He ducked through a low doorway and came to a toga-clad man behind a desk. The bald man looked up from his scrolls and his dull eyes raked down Volkard in a slow sweep. His round head held overly large brown eyes and a mouth too small for his face.

"What do you want?" the man asked. There was neither anger

nor excitement in his tone.

"I come to determine the likelihood of opening an inn here?"

The bald man sighed and turned from his desk to the many squared holes laden with scrolls behind him. His fingers searched the columns and rows for a few minutes pulling out a scroll now and then before slipping it back. At last he retrieved one, turned to his desk, and unwound it over the other documents strewn across the surface. "There are currently no inns in the city so you will have no competition. Do you have citizenship paperwork?" he asked again as his gaze swept over Volkard once more.

Volkard handed him the papers Arturos had provided.

The official scanned them and handed them back. "Where do you plan to house this inn? How many rooms and beds?" His monotone voice held as little life as a fish gasping for air on the shore.

"I wish to use the former inn just south of the city gate. It has five rooms with space to grow."

The man's head shot up and his large eyes bulged from his head—yet there was still no life in his voice. "Why there?"

"It was already an inn. There are minor repairs to be made but nothing structural. The biggest expense will be the furnishings."

The man tipped is head with a shrug of one shoulder, as if conceding to Volkard's wisdom. He looked down at his scroll again, and added something below the last line. "What do you intend to call this place?"

How could he name the place of his torment? The words tumbled over his lips. "Tutus Portum."

The man didn't raise his head but angled his eyes up. "Safe

Haven?" Another shrug, and he recorded it. The man sighed and put out his hand. "The Roman Empire requires forty denarii for the purchase of the inn."

Volkard's jaw slacked. He had talked to a few merchants and a couple of business owners on the way through the city. The price this official gave him was less than a third of what Volkard had expected.

"Fine. If you can pay me today, I will take thirty."

Volkard reached for his bag as his heart pounded near in his throat. "Agreed." He dropped the required price on the desk. *Great things You are doing, Lord.*

The man scooped it up and scribbled on the scroll. "Payment of taxes is due at the end of each month."

Volkard thought he was going to have to lean against a wall as he staggered under what God was doing. This was the last day of the month. He wouldn't owe any taxes for thirty days.

"This is the last day of August. The first taxes, of fifteen percent, are due at the end of October," the man droned as he recorded.

Not one month—but two. *Lord Almighty, great things You do!*

Volkard stumbled away in awe a few moments later, certain the sky would fall from the heavens any moment. But the blue firmament hovered securely overhead as he staggered back to the market square and purchased the supplies he would need to prepare the place. An axe, hammer, and small saw to make the furniture. A sickle to cut the tall grass outside and cloth to sew the mats and bedcoverings. Finally, a few cups and plates and he purchased a couple of the wooden trays like those in his dream.

And of course, he would need a few food items. He tossed what he could in the bag Arturos had given him and slung it over his shoulder, stacked the rest under his arm, and headed back to what was now his home.

It didn't make sense. No matter what he purchased, he had enough coin remaining in his pouch. It reminded him of a story Marcellus told him of a woman visited by a prophet. She only had a little oil; but after the man left, the jar of oil was full. Every time she poured some out, the jar remained full.

Volkard glanced to the heavens. "Thank You," were the only words that came to mind.

Halfway between the city gate and the inn, he saw the donkey on the road. Its head raised sniffing the air in his direction.

"Are you looking for me, Ol' Man?"

The donkey let out a long mournful cry as he trotted closer. He rubbed his muzzle against Volkard's arm as they walked.

"I'm back, you crazy beast. Calm yourself before you make me drop everything. I should have brought you with me to carry this load." He pushed past the animal and continued to the back door of the inn—the donkey remained close. "Hope you're still happy after I put you to work," Volkard chuckled, patting the donkey.

His smile slipped as his gaze fell again on the tree-covered hill poking above the inn. The final resting place of *her* ashes. He would look at it every day until God called him. There was no doubt in his heart, this would be his final home. He swallowed down the tears. Soon he would have to summon the courage to go and make peace with *her* and the haunting spot that would forever be his neighbor. Soon, but not just yet.

CHAPTER

THIRTY-NINE

Volkard ran his hands over his face. He hadn't taken a razor to his jaw since he left the gladiator school. He felt a little more like a man in control of his life each day as he labored and followed the Lord's leading. After a quick meal, he ventured into the woods on either side of the inn and continued felling slender young trees. After tying the cleaned trunks off, he had the donkey pull them to the back of the inn. There were better trees across the road, but death lay there. Volkard would only enter that area once—to say his final good-bye. And today was, again, not that day.

In fact, in the last few weeks, there had never been a day to return to the site where he lost *her*. Volkard constructed all the bed frames for the inn's five rooms, rehung the front door, replaced the shutters, and now worked on fashioning a new back door.

Each morning he opened the front door and looked across the road to the trailhead that led to where he needed to go. But when his heart wrenched until it doubled him over, he would turn and busy himself with projects until he dropped exhausted on his bedroll. He could not face completing his vow. Saying good-bye would be an end. Until then, there would still be one more time to be near where *she* lay. Another opportunity to meet with *her* in some way. But there would only be one more.

Things were changing. Over the last couple of mornings, focusing on work had become a struggle he couldn't bear. He thought of *her* constantly. Her warm sun-kissed skin, her smile, her long dark braid. He ached for her deeper than he dreamed possible.

This morning, he braced himself against the doorframe and stared out at the trees mocking him. The breeze ruffled the leaves. *Do that which you have promised, My son.*

Volkard raised his head, scanning everything within sight. He put one halting foot in front of the other until he stood in the middle of the road and looked both directions. As he feared, there was not another soul to be seen. God gave the direction. He needed to comply.

Do that which you have promised, My son.

Volkard trudged back to the inn, secured the door, and turned back to the woods. "I will go, Lord, but You must help me."

Volkard wandered much of the day, stumbling on shaking legs, unshed sobs burning the back of his throat. His heart and lungs wrapped in bands of regret. He staggered and dropped near the stream he remembered. *She* had knelt here where his knees now rested. Her hand had dipped in this cold water that bit at his fingers now. "Christus, I miss her, and we had no time to even know one another."

I am with you. Never will I leave you or forsake you.

Volkard faced the rising slope where the charred ruin, once called Sanctuary, still lay hidden far-off among the trees. He passed a boulder he thought *she* had leaned against to rest and ran his hand over the rough surface. It scratched at his skin like the ache rubbing a hole in his soul. "Please, Lord, can't I go back?"

Be strong and courageous. Do not fear because of this.

Dense forest met him and, after almost an hour, he realized he had taken a wrong turn. After another two hours he found the boulder again and started out once more. But he still could not find the trail. Back to his marker, he searched in ever growing circles finding another large rock near another trail at the foot of a different rise. He sat resting weary muscles before starting out once more.

He lost his way a couple of more times. Leaning against a tree, he looked toward the descending sun. "Christus, I can't do this. I can't let *her* go."

My son, I can do immeasurably more than you ask or dream. Trust Me.

As the last rays of the sun warmed his back, he came into the clearing he sought and dropped to his knees.

The setting sun glowed over the ghostly shell of the burned-out meetinghouse. It looked to still be ablaze, and Volkard again heard her cries. He buried his face in his hands and choked. Within that building she had sat beside him on a bench—long since turned to ash—and eaten her meals while smiling often at him. Oh, how he wished then, as now, he could have shared words with her. What was *she* thinking? What did *she* like and why? He had been so close to *her,* and yet they were worlds apart.

The men's huts listed and some had fallen down the steep slope. *She* had met him almost every morning outside the hut he shared with another man. He had forgotten his name. Volkard could see *her* still as he opened the door. *Her* smile more radiant than the rising sun behind *her.*

The women's huts on the right looked in better shape. Two still stood—one had been *hers.*

His heart so heavy he had to crawl, he moved to her old hut and tried to enter it. The wild creatures had stripped the beds of their soft insides, but Volkard knew *her* scent lingered within the walls. It reminded him of balsam, a purple flower that grew wild in much of Germania's high peaks.

Half in the hut and half out, Volkard collapsed in a heap. His heart rent in two and shattered into a million deadly shards. *Why did I come here? There is nothing but death and loss—beyond what I can bear.*

CHAPTER

FORTY

Musty soil filled his nostrils. Hard packed earth provided no comfort to his aching body. Sleep avoided him, leaving Volkard a shell of himself on the floor of *her* old abandoned hut. He begged the Lord, "Let me take my last breath. Here. Now. Let me be released from this life to join *her*—and You, Christus. Please." Joining *her* was his only desire. To hear *her* words that sang in his ears though he hadn't been able to understand them. To bathe in *her* smile. To float in *her* gaze. This was the cry of his heart.

Trust Me.

After a time, neither death nor sleep saved him from the pain, so he pushed to his knees and rubbed his hands over his face. He brushed dirt and twigs from his beard.

As he leaned back and gazed at the stars blinking out in the dim glow of the rising sun, he knew. "You did not save me from death and dying in the arena to let me die here. As much as I wish it. You have a bigger purpose for me."

Again, a whisper danced on the breeze. But now it felt almost giddy. *Trust Me.*

Volkard pushed to his feet and stretched his aching muscles, but as he turned to the burned-out shell—to at last put words to his farewell—movement high on the hill to his right caught his eye.

At the crest of the hill, above the abandoned camp, a silhouetted figure moved between the trees caught in the first rays of sunlight filling the sky. The profile of a woman, slender—but with a pleasing form. A braid swished across her back.

Volkard's heart slammed so hard he stumbled forward. Her spirit still wandered here. She was not in paradise as he hoped.

"Salomeh!" The word tore from his throat unbidden.

The phantom turned as though she heard him. Her shoulders trim above her narrow waist. Her ghostly skirt billowing in an otherworldly breeze. She stood still, as if waiting for the words he had come to bring her.

Pain, regret, and loss tore them from his throat and the German words splashed to the ground with his tears. "Oh Salomeh. Forgive me. I am sorry I ever invaded your world and brought you such pain." He bowed his head, unable to look at her ghost still trapped in this hateful place. "Christus, take her to Your side. Don't let her spirit languish here."

As he looked up again, she was gone.

He staggered, trying to stay upright. The weight of his loss, somehow heavier than before. He couldn't breathe. Thought and reason fled him. His gaze searched the crest for any sign she might have remained—though he didn't want her to and wished she would never leave at the same time.

Snap!

Crash!

Rip!

Volkard blinked at the sounds growing in his ears. Soldiers

coming again to carry him away? A wild forest beast racing to devour him? They could have him.

The commotion grew. The forest litter crushed. The light from the rising sun slipped farther down the slope—but not enough to see what charged at him.

Footfalls. Running, charging. Footfalls coming at him.

The sun rose another degree bathing his attacker in a mist of light. Braid flying. Skirt hem pulled up. Ten steps from him, she gasped. Five, she dropped her skirt. Three, she threw out her arms and launched herself at him.

A solid form slammed into him driving him back several steps before he dropped. Warm quivering arms wrapped around his neck. Balsam scent filled the air. A smooth cheek pressed against his. And the voice of an angel danced by his ear.

"Volkard, life is are us," she stuttered in German.

He froze, then as reality caught up to his thoughts, laughter burst from him in a roar of joy he could not control.

She pulled only a little from him to look into his eyes. Deep brown eyes, he believed he would never see again. Yet here they were caressing his face in wonder.

"Your German is still atrocious," he laughed.

"Oh Volkard," she gasped laying both her hands on either side of his face. "You are alive. And you speak Latin!"

He took one of her hands and kissed her palm. He pressed his forehead against hers as she knelt in the grass between his knees. "And, thank Christus, you are alive as well." He turned to look at the burned-out building. "But how did you survive?"

She leaned back following his gaze and shuddered. She moved

to sit beside him. Her arm looped in his and head resting against his shoulder. "We were trapped inside. The fire coming at us from both sides and the front." A tremor raged through her.

Volkard wrapped his arm around her and pulled her closer. She tucked her head under his chin. Her shaking lessened.

"As the smoke filled the room, Sammanus was there with us, but most of the other men were outside with you."

Volkard remembered the grey-haired man who cared for the people of the Sanctuary and the sight of the men who either lay dead or chained with him that day.

"Sammanus prayed and prayed. The building shifted as the flames ate away at its strength. A board in the back corner cracked. Sammanus and Martha kicked at it until a hole was created for us to slip through." She shuddered again. "We wiggled through as fast as we could…"

Volkard rubbed his hand down her arm still marveling that he cradled her in his embrace.

"Lyvia and Peter did not escape." Tears dripped on him. "But…" She raised her arms and pushed up her sleeves revealing the white-splotched burn scars on her skin. "Still the Lord—" The words broke off, and she pulled from him. She stared at him as though he had grown two heads in the moments since she last looked at him. "What did you say?"

"When? While I called to you?"

She shook her head. "You said we were both alive by…"

He smiled at her. "The grace of an almighty, loving God. The God who died to save me. Christus."

She threw her arms around his neck and squealed.

CHAPTER

FORTY-ONE

Volkard reveled in the warmth of the living, breathing woman he loved as she pressed to his chest wrapped in his arms.

"You must tell me everything!" She sat back to look at him, hands on his arms. "The last I saw of you, they beat you to the ground and put chains on you. Where did they take you? How did you escape? And how did you come to trust the Savior?"

Volkard told her of being chained to the relentless Marcellus. Of being marched to the ludus, and Marcellus joining him. "He said it was proof that Christus wished to have me." Volkard chuckled, though sadness tugged at his heart. "For such a skinny, small man to be bought to be trained as a gladiator was all the proof I should have needed, Marcellus told me repeatedly."

"Did he die in the arena?" she asked brushing a couple of scars on his face with her finger.

"He would not fight and kill another. He said he knew where he was going and had the hope of seeing his family and the God he loved. He would not kill another and damn them to an eternity without the same opportunity. He made sure he died in his first bout."

"But you…"

A smile touched his lips and again he took her hand and kissed her palm. "Marcellus spoke a prophecy over me, early in our training. 'You will leave this place alive, and there will be no blood on your hands.' I held to that promise when I gave my life to Christus after Marcellus died."

He told her of the beating and being Arturos' teacher in the Way as he healed in the cave under the ludus. And how, after his old master became his brother, he had been set free—as the Lord had promised.

Holding her hand, a thought struck him, stealing his breath. "I haven't seen you in two years, Salomeh. Surely a man has—surely you are no longer alone." The words squeezed through his aching throat.

She pulled her hand from his and moved a few inches away. Light fled from her eyes. "No. My heart was stolen from me. I did not have it to offer to any other." She bit at her lower lip. "But I feared he was forever lost to me,"—she shrugged—"perhaps he has forgotten about me and found another himself."

Volkard seized her by the shoulders ready to shake her. "There has never been, nor will there ever be, any other for me but you, Salomeh."

She rose tall on her knees. Her hands slid over his shoulders, and her fingers laced in his hair. Her head tipped and her lips hovered over his. He could taste her breath. "There has never been, nor will there ever be, anyone for me but you, Volkard."

Snap!

Volkard leapt to his feet pulling her up with him. He spun, scanning the slope below to find the noise. Someone approached, crunching through the woods. He pulled from her, "Run, Salomeh." He tried to push her away.

She stepped beside him, seizing his hand with the strength as fierce as any gladiator and laced her fingers in his. "No."

He opened his mouth to plead with her, but she spoke first.

"I thought I lost you once, and it nearly destroyed me. I will not leave you again. We either run together or stand together. Which will it be?"

Volkard stood frozen in a storm of emotions. His overwhelmed heart threatened to break the confines of his chest. Yet his gut wrenched with the vision of losing her at the very moment he found her. The world stopped.

Until a figure stepped out of the brush. It threw back its shaggy head and let out a long ear-splitting bray.

Volkard released a gust of air trapped in his lungs and braced himself on his knee with his free hand. "Are you following me, Ol' Man?"

The donkey called several times bobbing its head.

"You know this creature?" Her words danced with laughter.

"I saved his life, and it seems he hates to be parted from me."

She unwound their fingers and slipped her arms around him. Her head rested on his shoulder. "I know the feeling."

"It went this way." The voice of a man came toward the clearing.

"Tell me again, why we are following a dumb donkey that has no value?" another asked.

Salomeh looked up at Volkard, her brow raised in question.

CHAPTER

FORTY-TWO

Volkard never ran from a fight—ever. But he was not the man he was. God had miraculously reunited him with Salomeh. She stood beside him as men approached. Memories bombarded him of what happened last time outsiders came into this place. Wisdom told him to hide. Run and hide her, stay with her, stay alive *with her*.

He pointed past the old huts. As they moved silently to the brush, he waved the donkey away, mouthing words the animal could not understand.

He lifted Salomeh over a fallen tree twice as big around as he. She nestled in its shadow, back pressed to the bark, and he lay beside her, shielding her with his body. She tucked her head under his chin and clutched his tunic. He heard her voice barely the sound of a bee's buzz.

"Lord, You have blessed us. We trust You to keep us safe together."

As her head rested on his elbow, he draped his other arm over her and cradled her.

The voices of the men came into the clearing. "See, I told you it came this way."

The donkey rutted in the leaf litter some distance away.

"What is this place?" a different voice said.

"Some of the followers of that religion, the Way, thought they could hide from Rome's legions."

"I see we disappointed them."

Volkard tightened his hold as she trembled.

"Is there ever a doubt? The trained might of Rome against a simpering group who say they follow a God of love." The man snorted and the others' laughter joined in.

"All right, Tarus, I have followed your four-legged folly long enough. The beast has no owner, is old, and of no value, and there is no one here any longer needing the Emperor's justice. Can we please return to barracks now? I am hungry and need a bath."

"Very well."

Their footsteps faded, but Volkard did not move. *What if they only play at going away only to jump out on us as we emerge?*

Volkard clung to Salomeh. Only an hour ago he believed he would never see her again. Her body was warm and soft against his as each breath caressed his collarbone. Her heart beat so strong he could feel it on his chest. She released his tunic, but her hand remained. She did not wiggle free but melted into him.

The scent of spring wild-flowers consumed him. And the vision of the inn visited him again.

Now he recognized the voice that called a welcome to the family. But while the mother set aside her child this time, she did not take only his hand. Now he saw clearly, she grasped both his hand and another hand—one the color of honey, marked by a white scar.

Salomeh stood beside him radiating love—to the woman and her family.

I can do immeasurably more than you ask or dream.

Volkard released her, flopped to his back and stared up at the brilliant blue sky—bluer than it had ever been. "Thank You, Lord."

Salomeh rose up from the niche where she hid. She caressed his face. Her thumb brushed a scar over his left brow. Her smile could not be contained. "Yes, indeed. We thank You, Father, for great things have You done."

Her fingers slipped into his hair, and she pulled his head to her. Her lips brushed his—gentle and tentative.

He wrapped his arm around her and pulled her closer. She deepened the kiss. He cradled her head and answered her passion that drank deep of her lips. He skimmed down her jaw until he reached the tender spot below her ear. She moaned.

Bray!

Salomeh yelped as she sat up. Her dress scraped across the bark of the fallen tree. She pushed the donkey's muzzle off her shoulder where he nipped at her dress. "Stop that."

Volkard propped up on one elbow, but failed to cover his laughter with a sharp order. "Listen here, Ol' Man. You better get used to sharing me; for I will not again be parted from this woman."

Leaning forward she kissed him again, "Nor I from you." She whirled to glare at the donkey who tried to bite at her again. "We need to make peace, you and I."

The donkey tossed its head, snorted, and ambled off.

CHAPTER

FORTY-THREE

Salomeh pulled him to his feet. "Come."

"Where are we going? The inn is the other way."

"I know, but first we go to Matthew."

He stopped her. "Who is Matthew, and why must we go to him?"

"He leads us now. Sammanus went to the Father last year. And I cannot disappear without telling them where I have gone. They would worry and search for me. It would put them in danger."

"How long will we stay?"

A blush tinted her cheeks. "Not long."

Did it matter? Salomeh was alive and loved him. He would go anywhere to remain with her. Their fingers entwined as they now moved up the slope she had careened down earlier to leap into his arms. His chest still throbbed from the impact—or was that the love now filling the place where his brokenness had lain?

Volkard called to the mangy donkey. "Ol' Man, we are going this way. You coming?"

It bobbed its head and ambled after them.

"It's like he can understand you." She leaned into his arm.

"It is an odd thing to be sure."

At the far side of a second large hill, Volkard stopped her. She panted for breath, "Rest a minute."

"I'm fine," she protested.

He gathered her into his arms and kissed the top of her head. "Then allow the donkey a moment to catch up." The old creature came through the brush half way up the hill.

She pressed against him, resting her cheek on his chest. "Very well." She sighed contentedly.

Glancing around, Volkard asked, "Where is this new home of yours?"

She didn't release her hold around him but inclined her head in the direction they had been travelling. "Two more hills that way."

He put his hands on her shoulders and held her at arm's length.

She pouted.

"What time did you leave to be on the crest of the hill at day break? And why did you come?"

She smiled—that smile that made everything right in his world and warmed his very soul. "I lay on my bed last night, but I couldn't be still. It was as if stinging ants had infested it. I got up and started walking. I felt God calling to me—singing to me of wonders and things I could not understand. I simply followed. With the sunrise, I saw where I had ended up, I was angry with the Lord. To use such beauty to call me to a place of such hate and fear." Her face hid from him for a moment. "I am ashamed to admit I was scolding God for being cruel." Her face turned toward him again, and her eyes filled with wonder. "Then I heard it. My name carried on the wind with a hint of the German tongue coloring it.

"I could not believe my ears. I stopped and held my breath. I didn't dare believe…. Then it came again that most beautiful sound of my name followed by a long string of German that broke my heart but could only have come from my barbarian hero." She caressed his face. "Why did you come? You thought I was dead. What did you say to me?"

"I came to apologize for all the pain I caused you. For ever having come into your life at all."

Her hand that so tenderly stroked his face pulled back into a fist to pop him in the arm.

Volkard rubbed the spot. "What was that for?"

She wagged her finger at him for a moment, "Volkard of the German tribes, and stealer of my heart, don't you ever again say such a thing. I forbid you to be sorry for taking me that day." She softened, cradling his face with both hands. "For it was that day, I fell in love with you." She pressed her lips against his and wrapped her arms around his neck, holding him tightly.

As she relinquished his mouth he said, "And I you, Salomeh."

CHAPTER

FORTY-FOUR

Late in the afternoon, Salomeh led him into the new Sanctuary. Their huts were hidden among the trees and the central meeting place was a branch-covered tent not a recognizable building.

"Friends come, share in our joy. God has returned Volkard." She waved a greeting.

People streamed from the tree line and clamored to them.

A woman took his arm. "Vertex, is he with you? Do you know what became of him?"

A man's hand landed on his shoulder, "Augustus? My son, is he still alive?"

Several more pelted him with questions of their loved ones, until he shook free and put up his hands. "I am truly sorry. I know nothing of those you have lost. We were bound in chains and marched several days to a Roman post. There they separated us, and I did not see them again." His heart broke for them. He knew their pain. It was his own only this morning. Why had God allowed him of all people to return? He was the least deserving.

Salomeh looped her arm in his. "God has done a wonder. I pray He will do the same for each of you. I grieve your loss."

"As do I," Volkard added as the others left. He looked at

Salomeh. "We did not think what our joyous news would do to them."

"I know. It was unkind—but no less joyous." She smiled up at him and left his side as two men approached.

The elder, a man whose dark hair had strands of grey, extended his hand. "Welcome brother, I've heard a great deal about you." His head tipped toward Salomeh who was now surrounded by women. "There were times I thought you an angel of her imaginings—she spoke of you with such awe." He chuckled. "I am Matthew." He released Volkard's hand.

"Thank you, Matthew. I never thought to see her again. God has overwhelmed me with His love."

"And you think you are good enough for her?" A short man next to him sneered. Volkard recognized him from his time living with them before—but couldn't remember his name.

"I am quite sure I am not. But the Lord has brought us together for a purpose."

"And what might that be, barbarian?"

The word on this man's lips sounded nothing like how Salomeh had said it earlier as they journeyed here.

"Silas," With a gentle hand Matthew steered the man away. "That will be enough. The wood needs stacking."

Silas shot Volkard a glare and limped away. Volkard didn't remember him having an injury.

"Forgive him. He favored Salomeh, but she could not be wooed with such a broken heart."

Volkard nodded. He imagined any man would be smitten by her beauty and could not fault him for admiring her.

"Now, walk with me and tell me of the purpose the Lord has given you."

"The inn, outside the city gate. The one used as a haven for brothers and sisters seeking refuge from the hate of Rome."

Matthew nodded, his hands laced behind his back.

"The last couple was killed for their godly work, and the place has remained in ruins since. The Lord has called me to reopen it. And He has shown me working with Salomeh at my side."

Matthew stopped and considered him. "She is to work alongside you?"

He inflected the question in an odd manner, making Volkard believe Matthew doubted his claim. "Yes, it is true. I have seen it."

"I cannot allow her to go with you."

"But the Lord has brought us together. He has ordained it."

A slim smile tickled at Matthew's lips as if Volkard missed something, and he clenched his fists.

"It would be improper to send her…"

"Improper? But God—" Volkard caught sight of Salomeh. She stood in a clean gown of light green with a ring of flowers on her flowing hair. Heat filled his cheeks, and he resented the embarrassment, but he had been thoroughly dull. "Matthew, would you allow my *wife* to come with me?"

A wide smile spread across his face. "If she has agreed to join her life to yours, then I can do nothing to stop her, my brother."

Salomeh rejoined them bringing the scent of flowers. "It is what I wish more than my very breath." She took his hand.

"Well, give the man a moment to make himself presentable, sister, and we will all gather for the joyous event.

CHAPTER

FORTY-FIVE

The inn hummed with occupants. People from the city came for meals, and travelers rented all the beds. Volkard hired a man to help him build additional rooms so they would turn away less people. He had already added two more tables to the gathering room, and others ate outside under the eaves.

Volkard set a pitcher of beer on one table and moved to the next with another. He moved out of the way where he could as Salomeh squeezed past with a tray of food. Her bulging belly brushed against him and they shared a smile.

They met in the kitchen a moment later. Wrapping his arms around her, he caressed her wide stomach. "You should be off your feet. The child will come soon." He kissed her temple.

She smiled. "Soon, my love but not today. We have customers aplenty, and the help we hired won't arrive until next week."

"Will you at least take a rest, beloved?"

"As soon as this crowd thins, you can find me on the stool outside, next to your cranky old donkey."

"Promise?"

She kissed him, "If you will come and sit with me, my love."

"I will sit beside you every day of my life, beloved."

GLOSSARY

Actus – land surveying measurement about 116 ft

Amphora (pl. amphorae) – liquid measurement about 7 gals

Atrium – the center of the house and domestic life

Arretium – city in Ancient Rome in northern Italy, conqured by the Romans in 311 BC (now Azzero) used as military station.

Auctorati – men who sold themselves to be gladiators for fame or to pay off debt

Braccae – pants warn by Roman cavalrymen

Calcei – outdoor leather, wrap low calf, footwear used throughout Rome.

Caldarium – (hot room) third step in bathing Roman style in a heated tank

Caligae- Roman solider sandals with nails in the soils for better traction

Coena libera – parties for the gladiators the night before the fight

Congius (pl. congii) – slightly less than a gallon

Culina – kitchen in Roman home

Denarii – Roman coins

Doctores – trainers of the gladiators

Eques – a lithe gladiator who fought from horseback

Frigidarium – (cold room) first step in bathing Roman style in a tank of cold water

Gladius – 27 inch short straight sword, broad towards the handle, designed to thrust and parry rather than to cut and slice

Germanic Wars – a series of wars between the Romans and various Germanic tribes between 113 BC and 596 AD.

Greave – a piece of plate armor for the leg between the knee and the ankle, usually composed of front and back pieces.

Hasta – six-foot lance used for thrusting

Hoplomachi – well built gladiators, heavily armored and therefore slow

Hypogeum – underground portion of the arena, used to hold staging, animals, prisoners, and gladiators until they were released before the crowds

Impluvium – a shallow pool sunk into the floor of the atrium to catch the rainwater

Janus – god of doorways and beginnings, seen as the chief guardian of the home

Lanista – manager of a Ludus (gladiator school)

Lares –spirits of the families ancestors and along with the household gods were worshipped every day in Roman homes

Libra (pl. librae) – Roman pound about ¾ of a pound

Limes – The Limes Germanicus (Latin for Germanic frontier) was a line of frontier (limes) fortifications that bounded the ancient Roman provinces, dividing the Roman Empire and the unsubdued Germanic tribes from the years 83 to about 260 AD.

Ludi Gladiatorium – gladiator schools (ludus- singular)

Medici – a doctor who accessed the medical condition of gladiators

Milia Passuum – Roman mile about 1618.5 yds

Nein – 'No' in German

Non – 'No' in Latin

Novicius – a new gladiator recruit

Ocrea – metal greave worn on the lower left leg

Parmula – a small, light bronze shield, usually round

Passus – closest Roman equivalent to a yard or meter about 4 ft

Pes (pl. pedes) – Roman foot about 11.65 inches

Primus palus – the top fighter of a gladiator school

Retiarii – (Net Fighters) a type of gladiator that wore little armor other than a helmet and fought with a trident and net.

Rudus – wooden training sword (often double the weight of a metal blade) / also given as a symbol of freedom

Secundus palus – the second best fighter of a gladiator school

Stadium (pl. stadia) – distance measured at sea about 607 ft

Strigil – a smooth sick used to strap oil and dirt from the body in a caldarium

Stola – a Roman woman's garment

Subligaculum – canvas loincloth worn by hoplomachi gladiators

Tablinum – the office in a Roman house

Tepidarium – (warm room) second step in bathing Roman style in a tepid tank

Tirones gladiatores or Tiro – trained gladiators ready to fight in the arenas

Trestle Table - A table of two supports linked by a long cross-member over which a board or tabletop is placed

Triclinium (plural: triclinia) – formal dining room in a Roman building

Uncia (pl. unciae) – Roman inch

Vesta –goddess of the hearth

Velites (Singular: Veles) – Roman Gladiator who fought on foot using a spear called a hasta.

Veteranus (Veterani) – gladiators who survived there first match

Villa Rustica – a farm-house estate permanently occupied by the servants who had charge generally of the estate. The villa rustica centered on the villa itself, perhaps only seasonally occupied.

Willkommen – welcome in German

About the Author

Michelle Janene (Murray) is a church secretary by day and writes Christian fantasy and historical fiction in all her free time. She lives in Northern California with two crazy dogs and the characters of her imagination.

If you enjoyed *Barbarian Hero* please leave a review on your favorite site.

You can connect with Michelle on:
You can connect with Michelle on:
Facebook: Michelle Janene or Strong Tower Press
Twitter: @MichelleJaneneM
Pinterest: www.pinterest.com/michellejanene
Goodreads: Michelle Janene
MichelleJanene.com
StrongTowerPress.com

Other Books

Check out these books also by Michelle

Mission: Mistaken Identity

The Changed Heart Series:
God's Rebel
Rebel's Son
Hidden Rebel

Seer of Windmere

Guardians of Truth

Culling a Miracle

Lost Stones

The Last Good King

Found in the Scars

The King's Vengeance

Thrice a Bride

Dragon Fire